MIDDLE SCHOOL
FIELD TRIP FIASCO

James Patterson is the internationally bestselling author of the highly praised Middle School books, *Katt vs. Dogg, Ali Cross* and the I Funny, Jacky Ha-Ha, Treasure Hunters, Dog Diaries and Max Einstein series. James Patterson's books have sold more than 385 million copies worldwide, making him one of the biggest-selling authors of all time. He lives in Florida.

Martin Chatterton was born in Liverpool, England, and has been successfully writing and illustrating books for over thirty years. He has written dozens of books for children and illustrated many more, collaborating with a number of illustrious authors along the way, including several British Children's Laureates. His work has been published in fourteen languages and has won or been shortlisted for numerous awards in the UK, US, and Australia. As Ed Chatterton, Martin writes crime fiction, screenplays and historical fiction and several of his books are in development with various TV and film producers. After time spent in the US, Martin now divides his time between Australia and the UK.

Since graduating with a first-class degree in graphic design from the Liverpool School of Art, **Anthony Lewis** has illustrated more than 500 children's books for publishers around the world. His titles include the Smarties Prize-winning *The Owl Tree* by Jenny Nimmo and *Atticus the Storyteller's 100 Greek Myths* by Lucy Coats, shortlisted for the Blue Peter Book Award. He works in a variety of styles on everything from the simplest baby board books to large anthologies for both the fiction and non-fiction markets. He lives in a small Cheshire village with his wife Kathryn, a graphic designer who has designed a number of the books he has illustrated, and their three children, Isabella, Emilia, and Rory.

MIDDLE SCHOOL
FIELD TRIP FIASCO

JAMES PATTERSON
AND MARTIN CHATTERTON

ILLUSTRATED BY ANTHONY LEWIS

1 3 5 7 9 10 8 6 4 2

Young Arrow
20 Vauxhall Bridge Road
London SW1V 2SA

Young Arrow is part of the Penguin Random House group of companies
whose addresses can be found at global.penguinrandomhouse.com

Penguin
Random House
UK

First published in Great Britain by Young Arrow in 2021

Based on *Middle School: Going Bush*, published in Australia by
Random House Australia Children's in 2016

www.penguin.co.uk

A CIP catalogue record for this book is available from the British Library

ISBN 9781529119909

Printed and bound in Great Britain by Clays Ltd, Elcograf S.p.A.

The authorised representative in the EEA is Penguin Random House
Ireland, Morrison Chambers, 32 Nassau Street, Dublin D02 YH68

MIX
Paper from
responsible sources
FSC
www.fsc.org
FSC® C018179

Penguin Random House is committed to a
sustainable future for our business, our readers
and our planet. This book is made from Forest
Stewardship Council® certified paper

MIDDLE SCHOOL
SCHOOL
FIELD TRIP FIASCO

CHAPTER 1

BOREDOM IS THE WORST

Let me start out by saying, I did *not* expect my school art trip to end with someone breaking into my bedroom to steal the legendary Brilliant Bluebird Diamond. But that's *exactly* what happened.

Okay, let me back up, start at the beginning.

I'm Rafe Khatchadorian. You might've heard of me? I'm kind of famous from *Middle School, The Worst Years of My Life,* the bestselling book. (There's even a movie about me!)

You're probably wondering about that diamond thing I mentioned, aren't you? I'll get to that. But first, if you know anything about me, you won't be surprised that my art trip to California ended in complete and total disaster, but I swear I didn't mean for it to! In fact, I was doing pretty good before that. Not getting in trouble I mean. *How,* you ask? With the help of my friend, Flip Savage, only the coolest, funniest, most awesome kid ever.

We were spending all our free time playing video games. Mom wasn't exactly happy about that, but it was keeping me out of trouble, right?

And now Flip and I were on another mission: defeating the evil Bridge Troll blocking the Arch of Freedom!

"Rafe-ster, watch out!" Flip shouts.

I dodge a rock the troll threw at us. "What do we do now?" I ask.

"This shouldn't be that hard," Flip says. "There's one of it, and two of us!" He steps toward the Troll. It growls, oozing drool hanging from its razor-sharp teeth.

It lunges for us, and I brandish my sword. I'm like one of those movie heroes charging into battle. "Let us pass, you monster!"

"Neverrrr," it growls.

"Oh yeah?" I lunge, sword out.

"Rafe!" The Troll glares at me.

I raise my sword.

I charge the Troll.

Flip cheers me on. We're almost there—

"RAFE." Mr. Rourke stood over my desk. He looked down at my paper. Instead of taking notes, I'd drawn all over the page—trolls and bridges, and Flip and me as knights.

Oops. Busted.

I do that sometimes. Think about something more fun when I'm bored. I can't help it, it's just how my brain works. But with Mr. Rourke watching me, I had to shut my notebook. I had to leave the trolls and fighting behind, and come back to earth where I was stuck at school.

And it was the *worst*.

CHAPTER 2

FOUR REASONS THINGS AREN'T THE WORST

Okay, okay, not *everything* was crummy. For starters:

1. I got to see plenty of my mom and Grandma Dotty (even if I also had to deal with my annoying little sister, Georgia).

2. School was okay. There's no clever punchline here because, mostly, that's what school's like, right? Sort of somewhere between *okay* and *meh*. Not amazing, not terrifying, just kind of in the middle. Hey, maybe that's why it's called middle school? Har-har-har.

3. Junior! Dogs make everything better. Everyone should have a dog. In case you

haven't been keeping up with things (and if not, why?), this is Junior. I know I'm biased and you probably think your dog is the Best Dog of All Time but I'm here to tell you that you are just plain wrong. Junior is the Best Dog of All Time, that's all there is to it.

4. I was doing some seriously awesome art. I was filling my sketchbooks with a heap of new stuff. (Not all of it during class, I swear!) I hadn't shown them to anybody yet but I thought they were looking pretty good.

Great stuff, eh? Did you like that part where I became President of the United States and invaded Pluto? You did? BUSTED! There *was* no part where I became President of the United States and invaded Pluto. Now, go back and read the list properly.

So, yeah. All in all, life in Hills Village wasn't too bad. I was just *bored,* and that made me annoyed because I hate being bored. I mean, who likes it, right? But I couldn't do anything about it, and that was the real crummy part.

CHAPTER 3

PUSHING THE ENVELOPE

"Hi, honey. How was school?" Mom asked when I came home.

She was standing with her back to me, making pancakes, which filled the kitchen with the smell of, well, pancakes.

I shrugged and dumped my backpack by the door. Then Junior barked and jumped up for me to pet him. He was a good distraction from having to answer Mom. I bent down and scratched him behind the ear. He rolled onto his back. His tongue drooped out of his mouth.

"Who's a good boy?" I asked, rubbing his belly.

I could hear Grandma Dotty watching TV in the living room. She does a lot of that these days and sometimes talks to us about her favorite soap actors like they're real people. I've tried pointing out that they're not real, but now I just nod and agree with whatever she says.

There was no sign of Georgia. She was probably up in her room, arranging the world's biggest collection of stuffed animals. Georgia's got *a lot* of stuffed animals. Sometimes I think she'll go into her room and we'll just lose her in the crowd.

"Oh, I almost forgot," Mom said. "You've got a letter."

On the kitchen table was an envelope. It was

propped up very suspiciously against a potted plant. I sat down and looked at it like it might explode. The envelope, I mean—not the potted plant.

Rafe Life Lesson #22

Envelopes propped up on the kitchen table should be approached with

EXTREME CAUTION!

Suddenly, Mom having her back to me took on new meaning.

Did she already know what was in the envelope? Were the pancakes to soften the blow of bad news? I wondered if Principal Stricker or her evil minion, Vice Principal Stonehouse, had secretly signed me up for some other fiendish punishment: coal-mining in Alaska, or cleaning the inside of a Ukrainian radioactive fuel dump using only my tongue.

Mom turned around and waved her spatula at the envelope. "What's it say?"

I picked up the envelope. It was official-looking. So it probably wasn't a super-late (or super-early) Christmas card or anything safe like that.

Nope.

It was from my school.

SPROING! Georgia appeared out of nowhere. I wasn't surprised. She had a weird radar for any bad news coming my way.

"Are you going to open that or just stare at it?" she asked.

"No, I figured I'd stare at it some more," I said, rolling my eyes and hoping she would go away.

Georgia didn't go away. She kept snooping in my business, looking at the letter. I waited for Mom to turn back to the pancakes, then shooed Georgia away.

I was ready for the worst.

Worse than the worst. Whatever that is, I was ready for it. Just get this over with…

I ripped open the letter.

CHAPTER 4

THE LETTER

Dear Mr. Khatchadorian,

Every four years the Institute for the Advancement of Writers and Contemporary American Artists (IAWCAA) asks a select number of middle schools from around the country to recommend a promising young artist to take part in an educational arts trip. This year the trip will begin on April 27 and takes the form of a week-long "Camp Culture" in California. At the end of the week, there will be an art exhibit.

You have been selected to represent Hills Village Middle School in this all-expenses-paid opportunity. If you decide to accept our offer, please let us know by...

I stopped and reread the beginning. It still said the same thing.

A smile spread slowly across my face.

I, Rafe Khatchadorian, had been invited to an art field trip in *California*.

Me.

A "promising young artist"!

Just like that, a crummy day suddenly got a whole lot better.

Another chapter in the Adventures of Rafe Khatchadorian was about to begin...and I was going to make sure this one didn't end in disaster.

CHAPTER 5

EARTH TO RAFE

I played it cool.

"WOOOOOOOOOOOOHOOOOOOO!!!!!" I screamed, jumping around the kitchen.

Georgia stared at me like I'd lost my head. Junior looked like he was worried I'd step on him, so he hid under the table.

"What on earth...?" Mom dropped the jug of pancake mix on the floor.

But I didn't care.

I punched the air and spun in a circle.

"Khatchadorian shoots! He scores!" I shouted. "Good-bye, boring old reality. Hello, awesome California!"

"California?" Mom said.

I held out the letter and danced around the room. "Uh-huh, uh-huh!"

I probably looked a little silly, dancing around by myself. In my head, I pictured everyone joining in. Mom says, "This is amazing!" and starts dancing with me, holding the letter.

Junior starts running in circles around us. Then Grandma Dotty comes in and starts doing an old-lady move she calls the Twist.

We're having a big old dance party in the kitchen with balloons and streamers and loud music.

I do that dance step thing where you push out your arms and sort of run on the spot while singing a sentence over and over again. In my case that was: "I'm going to California, I'm going to California!"

Of course, that's when Georgia burst my bubble.

"Earth to Rafe!" she said, loudly. "You look stupid."

The party was gone. It was back to me, my mom, Georgia, and Junior in the kitchen. There were no balloons or streamers. And no fun music. No music at *all*.

"Keep the noise down in there!" Grandma Dotty yelled from the living room. "They're about to find out who the killer is!"

"The guy with the beard!" I yelled back. "It's always the guy with the beard!"

Mom stepped over Junior and sat down at the kitchen table. She still held the letter. "I don't know about this, Rafe."

Remember how I said I was ready for worse than the worst?

Guess I wasn't.

Because I wasn't ready for her to say *that*.

CHAPTER 6

HOUSTON, WE HAVE A PROBLEM...

What did she mean, *I don't know about this*?!
THIS just happened to be the best thing to happen to me!

THIS was the opportunity of a lifetime!

THIS was going to be amazing, epic, awesome, super, fantastic—the best *ever*!

She couldn't just...*not let me go*. I'd been specially selected for an *art* trip. This wasn't fair, Mom wasn't fair, life wasn't fair!

"This is so—" I began, ready to tell Mom exactly how unfair this was, when something really weird happened: I did something smart.

It was like there was a voice in my head telling me to *not* do the thing I was just about to do—that is, throw a complete, full-on tantrum, stomp off to my room, and sulk for a couple of days.

That won't get you what you want, said the voice.

Be smart.

I knew exactly what to do.

I hopped over Junior lying on the floor and grabbed my backpack. I yanked out my sketchbook. "Aha!" I held it up.

Georgia rolled her eyes at me and started petting Junior.

"I have to go, Mom," I said. "See?" I handed her my sketchbook. It's filled with all my drawings from the past few months. I'm pretty proud of them. Not to sound stuck-up, but some are really good. Like the one of my principal as a huge, scaly dragon about to eat a group of kids in detention.

Those poor kids. Never stood a chance.

"Those are weird," Georgia announced.

"No one asked you," I told her.

"These are great, Rafe!" Mom said.

I grinned. And I made sure Georgia saw. She stuck out her tongue.

Mom's always loved my art, but this was the first time I knew that she wasn't just saying it because I was her kid. She was saying it because I was *good*. I could feel the difference.

I know I come off all ironic about stuff, but when it comes to art, I am actually dead serious. I don't want to sound all touchy-feely about it but… art was what I wanted to do for the rest of my life, one way or another.

I want to make art. This isn't just a hobby anymore.

I NEEDED to go on this art field trip.

"Thanks," I said. "So…?"

"It's just…" Mom set my sketchbook on the table. "How are you getting to California, Rafe? And who else is going? Will there be a teacher? There's so much this letter doesn't say."

"Too bad for you! You can't go!" Georgia laughed like a crazy person. Even Junior seemed to notice.

He gave her a weird look.

"Let's talk to someone at school about it!" I said. "Please, Mom?"

"All right," she said. "Let's talk to your principal."

Uh-oh.

I was *not* looking forward to a visit with Principal Stricker.

AKA the Fire-Breathing Dragon Lady who runs our school.

Yikes.

Well, it was nice knowing ya! Remember me when I'm gone.

CHAPTER 7

MOM VS. THE DRAGON LADY

Mom braved Principal Stricker the very next day. She marched into the death lair while I hung around outside for like ten years. *Mom isn't coming back,* I thought. *This is it. I've seen the last of her.*

I wondered if it was too late to break down the door and rescue her.

Yeah right. More like this:

I paced and chewed my nails like they were prime BBQ ribs. Just when I started looking around for someone else's nails to chew, the door to the office opened and Mom staggered out.

"You survived!" I cheered.

"Mrs. Donatello was the one who nominated you," Mom said.

"Yes, I did," came Mrs. Donatello's voice. I spun around and there she was—*poof*, like a genie. She was my art teacher a while back and pretty much the only teacher who saw me as more than just a walking failure.

"Thanks, Mrs. D!" I turned to Mom. "So can I go?"

"Well, it's paid for by the IAWCAA," she said, "and Mrs. Donatello will be chaperoning, so…"

I can't WAIT. California...where they make all the movies!

Hollywood, here I come!

I wonder if I'll see any famous movie stars.

Or get to see a red carpet premiere...

Oh man! It was gonna be—

"Rafe, are you listening to me?" Mom asked.

I nodded. If you're going to lie, better not to say anything. Harder to get caught that way.

"You have to promise you'll be careful," she said. "No being—"

"Being my usual self?"

"No. Just don't get your usual self into trouble."

"Yeah, yeah—got it!"

"I'm serious, Rafe. No trouble." She kept talking and I kept nodding. But I wasn't listening.

Hey, would *you* be listening when you'd just

gotten the A-OK to go to *California* for an *art* trip???

Yeah. Didn't think so.

I would've agreed to a head transplant without anesthesia if that meant I could go. Luckily, I didn't need to.

I also didn't manage to stay out of trouble.

But if you know me—and by now I figure you do—you won't be surprised by that. Like I said at the beginning of this whole thing, it ends with a stolen diamond.

The famous Brilliant Bluebird Diamond, in fact, which had recently gone missing from one of the US's biggest museums. Somebody snuck in and stole it right out from under all the high-tech security, like a real-life Pink Panther. (You know, from that movie with the bumbling detective.) But then it went missing *again* because the thieves lost it in the middle of the desert! Yup, pretty embarrassing.

But in my story, there's no flamingo-colored jungle cat, just a crocodile who *definitely* almost ate me.

Okay, okay. I'm jumping ahead again. Before all that, I had to...

Drumroll *please*!

...

...

...

PACK!!!

Packing is *bor-ing,* though, so I'll be nice and get to the good stuff fast. To sum it up:

1. I packed furiously.
2. Had a Grade-A Meltdown because I couldn't find my ABSOLUTE FAVORITE T-shirt.
3. Found my ABSOLUTE FAVORITE T-shirt exactly where it should be, wadded up in a ball with all my other T-shirts.
4. Slept through my alarm.
5. Realized I was really, *really,* REALLY going to miss Junior when I tried to say good-bye.
6. Realized I really, *really,* REALLY wasn't going to miss Georgia when she said, "I can't wait to see what it's like to be an only child!"
7. Grandma Dotty got a speeding ticket on the way to the airport.

Grandma Dotty, driving at
the speed of light...

8. Then I WAS THERE. At the airport!

Oh yeah, but before all that? I had THE BEST
idea.

I know you don't believe me. You're thinking, *I
know Rafe. This idea* won't *be good,* much less *THE
BEST.* But trust me. It *was* a good idea! The best
ever. It's not my fault no one else thought so.

CHAPTER 8

DOGS ARE NOT ALLOWED IN SUITCASES (WHO KNEW!?)

Rafe," Mom said as we loaded my things into the car outside our house. "Why do you have two suitcases?"

"I have a lot of stuff?"

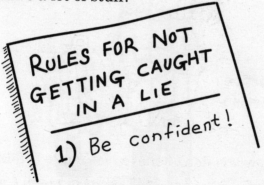

RULES FOR NOT GETTING CAUGHT IN A LIE

1) Be confident!

"Rafe..." She crossed her arms and gave me her Mom Look.

You know what that is. But if not, I'll tell you:

It's when your mom—or parent, or any adult, really—looks at you and they don't even have to SAY anything, you just *know* they're mad.

Usually it comes with crossed arms.

Also a scowl.

And looking down their nose at you.

Oh, plus, there's sometimes a bonus and it comes with annoying little sisters in the background glaring at you like you stole their favorite stuffed animal and then set it on fire.

Scowl ✓

Looking down the Nose ✓

Crossed Arms ✓

Angry Little Sister ✓

"Would you like to tell me what's really in the suitcase?" Mom asked. "Or should I open it and see?"

"Yeah," Georgia said. "And by the way, where's Junior, *Rafe*?"

I didn't answer. The suitcase wriggled.

Mom sighed and opened my second suitcase.

Out popped Junior, his tongue hanging out of his mouth.

"Woof!" he barked (I'd like to think he was telling Mom and Georgia that they'd ruined everything), then he jumped out of the back of the car.

"Rafe," Mom said in That Tone.

That tone that meant she was disappointed in me.

"I know, I know." I hung my head as I climbed into the car. "No more trouble. Got it."

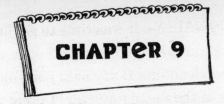

CHAPTER 9

AAAAAAND WE'RE OFF AND FLYING

At the airport, we met up with Mrs. Donatello. And then we had to wait *foreeeeever* to board. I was pretty sure my ninety-ninth birthday was going to come and go before the plane even took off.

I think Rafe could get there faster if he walked.

Then—FINALLY—it was time to get on the plane.

Mom and Grandma Dotty both gave me very public hugs at the departure gate. I pretended to be embarrassed because there were a lot of people around. Plus Mrs. Donatello. But, and this is just between us so don't tell anyone...

Secretly, I was happy.

On the plane, I sat next to Mrs. Donatello and this lady who smelled like the perfume section in fancy clothes stores.

"So, Rafe," Mrs. Donatello said. "Are you excited?"

In fact, I was VERY excited. Like bouncing out of my seat excited. Like Christmas-as-a-little-kid excited.

But I shrugged and said, "Yeah." Playing it cool, remember?

"This will be a great opportunity for you," she said, smiling in that way adults do when they've seen through your act.

Since she already knew I was only pretending, I gave up on the whole "playing it cool" thing...

"It'sgoingtobeamazingandsocoolandIcan'twait-togettthereandmeeteveryoneand—"

I had to stop because I had to breathe. It felt like I'd just run a marathon.

Mrs. Donatello's smile got bigger. "Yes it will, Rafe." She pulled a book out of her suitcase. "I'm glad you're so excited."

I grinned and nodded a billion times.

I was going to *Hollywood,* where we'd stay in a fancy Hollywood hotel, probably with a pool, room service, a huge TV, and maybe even MOVIE STARS staying there, too.

I grabbed my sketchbook and started doodling. Me and Flip, this time in LA, taking on a big, ugly, hairy monster hanging on the Hollywood sign, ripping off letters and throwing them across the hill.

We use our jetpacks to dodge flying letters. Barely.

"What're we gonna do?" Flip shouts, ducking under a big *O.*

"Stop the monster! Save the world!" I yell back.

"Well, *yeah,*" he mumbles, "but *how?*"

Suddenly, this loud rumble interrupted my drawing and I found myself back on the plane, sitting next to Mrs. Donatello. She'd fallen asleep while reading and was snoring.

"ZzzZzzZzzz..."

I went back to my drawing, and then—

"ZZZZZZzzzZZZZZZZZZZzzzz..."

It got LOUDER.

When we got to California, it was like no time had passed at all!

We left in the afternoon, flew a bunch of hours—longer than the last Avengers movie!—and we still got there in the afternoon. Weird, huh? That's time zones for ya!

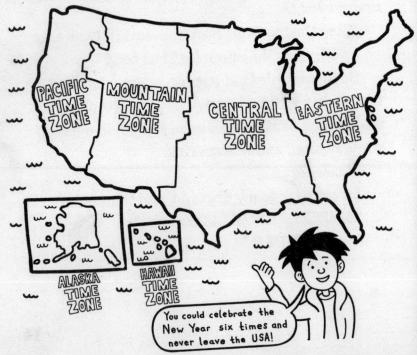

PACIFIC TIME ZONE

MOUNTAIN TIME ZONE

CENTRAL TIME ZONE

EASTERN TIME ZONE

ALASKA TIME ZONE

HAWAII TIME ZONE

You could celebrate the New Year six times and never leave the USA!

When we got off the plane, I thought we'd be able to see the Hollywood sign. But all I saw were a bunch of buildings. Not even a palm tree!

I also thought we'd take a taxi to the hotel. Instead, we got on a bus.

Nobody told me there'd be MORE traveling!

Just like nobody told me we'd be camping.

Yup! You heard that right.

CAMPING.

CHAPTER 10

GOOD-BYE, CIVILIZATION. IT WAS NICE KNOWING YOU!

I didn't sign up for this.

Then I remembered the letter had maybe sorta kinda mentioned something about... something.

I dug it out of my bag. I was at "Camp Culture," according to the letter.

Guess that's sneaky talk for YOU'RE GOING CAMPING, RAFE.

So long, Hollywood!

So long, movie star sighting!

So long, red carpet movie premiere!

It was fun while it lasted.

Oh, also, instead of being around movie stars, I found myself around country folk...

They were like those people you see on outdoorsy TV shows.

Example A: Johnno, our bus driver.

"What brings you folks to these parts?" he asked. But he didn't wait for us to reply. "Hear 'bout them cave paintings and want ter see for yerselfs?"

"Cave paintings?" I asked.

"I didn't know there were cave paintings around here," Mrs. Donatello said.

"Yeppers!" he replied. "Them cave paintings popped right up the other day, right in the mountain area known as Crocodile Rocks. No 'un's noticed 'em before, but suddenly—*boom*!"

Mrs. Donatello and I jumped.

"There's somethin' fishy goin' on over there," he said.

"Why is it called Crocodile Rocks?" I asked.

"Lots of 'em rocks out there look like crocs!"

"Cool." But I was pretty sure that was going to be about the only cool thing. Even some crocodile-shaped rocks couldn't make up for the *camping*.

But before we camped, we *did* get to stay in a hotel. If it can be called a "hotel"…

So long, civilization!

I mean, the place was called Bigbottom Creek!

I didn't see any creek, though, just miles and miles of nothing but sand. The road even became a dirt road after a while. When that happens, you just *know* you've gotten yourself into a mess. I didn't even have cell service!

After getting off the bus, we walked along this rocky path that was NOT good for rolling suitcases. Good thing Junior wasn't inside one. He'd have gotten jumbled around like laundry in a dryer.

I have to admit I felt kind of disappointed. It's not like I'd expected a marching band or anything—okay, maybe I *had* been expecting a marching band, or whatever the equivalent of a marching band was in Bigbottom Creek—but at least there could have been *some* kind of welcome.

Bigbottom Creek Hotel wasn't much of a hotel but it looked friendly...enough.

The guy behind the check-in desk directed us to a room at the back. "The reception's in there, folks," he said. "Just leave your gear with me and I'll stow it in your room."

The back room was packed and noisy with people chatting and eating. A man carrying a notebook looked like he was from a newspaper. Someone else was setting up a video camera next to a small stage. There were a bunch of guys in business suits talking to a guy with a big bushy beard. Everywhere you looked there were smiling people.

A woman with purple hair sitting behind a table near the door gave me and Mrs. Donatello name tags. "Grab a plate and dig in," she said, pointing to a long table piled high with food. "You're the last to arrive but there's plenty there."

Perfect. I was starving!

"Knuckles!" someone yelled from behind me.

Suddenly, I felt the kind of pain you get when someone rubs their knuckles right on the crown of your skull.

"OW!" I spun around, ready to defend myself, and came face-to-face with someone I never expected to ever see again.

CHAPTER 11

WELCOME TO BIGBOTTOM CREEK

So remember how I'm awesome and have all these awesome adventures? Of course you do! Well, one of my adventures was to Australia. Yep, the country down under.

Anyway, when I turned around, my friend from Australia, Ellie Watts, was grinning from ear to ear, her right hand bunched into prime knuckling position. She's just about the coolest person I've ever met.

She's awesome. She's smart, creative, and makes MOVIES!

She also once saved me from a nude surfing disaster (don't ask).

Even though things hadn't exactly worked out how we'd planned (because I'd ended up being chased out of Australia by a mob of angry zombies), it wasn't Ellie's fault.

Or Australia's.

But that's another story.

I stared at Ellie. I couldn't believe she was here!

"Sorry," she said in a voice that didn't sound even a tiny bit sorry. "Did that hurt?"

I rubbed the top of my head. It hurt like mad. "No," I lied. (Have you ever been knuckled? It hurts like *crazy*.)

"I can't believe you're here!" she said. "I missed you!"

"I missed you, too!"

Then she lunged at me. I thought she was about to knuckle me again, but she wrapped her arms around me, squeezing me in a death-hug that wasn't really much better. But it's the thought that counts. That's what Mom always says.

Breathing is overrated, right?

When Ellie finally let go, we stepped apart. I felt all hot in the face, especially as Ellie looked me up and down with her hands on her hips. "You didn't get any taller," she said.

"Yes, I did! You just got taller, too."

She shrugged like she didn't believe me. "Anyway, what're you doing here? Are you here for the art camp, too?"

Too? Did that mean...?

"'Cause that's what I'm here for," Ellie said.

"Me, too! But, I thought this was only for kids in the US?" Like I said, Ellie is from Australia, so

I wasn't really sure how she'd get to be part of this camp. Not that I mind—I was stoked she's here!—I was just confused.

"Well, I live here now." Ellie grinned. "Moved here a couple months ago. Pretty cool, huh?"

I nodded. "Very cool." I felt my face get hot again. Why didn't I come up with something better to say?

"Wanna hear something even cooler?" She leaned close and my legs went all weak and shaky.

You might want to get that checked out!

"Well?" she asked. "Wanna hear something even cooler?"

"Oh, uh, yes?"

"During the art camp, we're actually getting to see these neat cave paintings!"

"Huh?"

"There's a cave full of these old paintings," Ellie said. "And we get to check 'em out as part of our art trip."

"Oh, the middle-of-nowhere thing makes sense now." Maybe this trip wouldn't be so boring compared to Hollywood.

(Don't get me wrong: it would be abso-posi-lutely awesome to see Hollywood, but Ellie's here and we get to do art together, which is pretty awesome, too.)

"I think it's kind of nice out here," Ellie said.

"Oh, uh, yeah, I mean..."

She laughed as I turned red.

Rafe + tomato

= perfect color match

"Hey, no biggie," she said. "The outdoors isn't for everyone."

I started to sag with relief, until she added, "It's only for the tough people."

"I'm tough!"

She giggled. "If you say so."

"No, really—" I stepped back, trying to think of something to show her that I wasn't such a wimp, but I bumped into a large cardboard cutout. It was an ad for a TV show. It read: ALL-AMERICAN PAINTING AND FISHING SHOW STARRING BRUSHES MCGARRITY, FAMOUS DISCOVERER OF THE ROCKY HILLS CAVE PAINTINGS. ALL-AMERICAN PAINTING AND FISHING SHOW! EVERY MONDAY, 3:20 A.M., NBNBBC.

"Easy there!" someone said as I picked up the cutout. "Don't damage the publicity, kid."

I turned around to see the real-life version of the man on the cardboard cutout.

"Brushes McGarrity," he said, offering up a massive, gnarled hand. "Welcome to Bigbottom Creek, kiddo."

CHAPTER 12

I'M NOT MUCH OF A TALKER...

Brushes McGarrity smelled like paint and horses and looked like he'd been carved out of the ground Bigbottom Creek was built on: he was red, dusty, and wrinkled. He wore a full-length leather coat and a leather hat that matched his leather skin. His beard was made from wire and his teeth were a cheesy yellow. He couldn't have looked more country bumpkin if he'd been riding a tractor across a cornfield with a straw hat, a farmer's tan, and eating a tomato like it was an apple.

I shook Brushes' hand and tried not to show any pain as he mangled my fingers.

"This is the best little town in the whole of California!" Brushes said.

I thought that was a huge exaggeration. California has Hollywood!

"Welcome," he added, then peered at my name tag, "Ralph."

"Rafe," I said automatically, but Brushes had already gone.

He stepped up onto a little stage at one side of the room, put two fingers in his mouth, and blew a whistle that could be heard on the moon. "Gather around, everyone!" he yelled. "The last couple of folks have arrived, so we can get this shebang started.

"Now, most of you will know me from the All-American Paintin' and Fishin' TV show, or from my reputation as the dude who discovered the best collection of California cave paintings this side of LA. I'm here today in another role. Now, I'm not much of a talker, but I'm prouder than a parakeet to be hosting the first-ever Camp Culture. Thanks to the generosity of the Institute for the Advancement of Writers and Contemporary American Artists, Bigbottom Creek can now be..."

For someone who wasn't much of a talker, Brushes McGarrity sure could talk.

The rest of the night was all kinds of cool. I got interviewed by the local paper and someone took a bunch of photos of us all. I got to catch up with Ellie, too! Though...I was kind of making a fool of myself.

"—oh yeah," I was saying, "I do all kinds of cool stuff now, like..." *Think, Rafe, think!* "Like skydiving."

Ellie's eyebrows went so high they peeked over her glasses. "You went *skydiving*?"

"I mean, I, uh, I did say that..."

What was *wrong* with me? Why couldn't I talk to her without making things up? I didn't even want to lie, it just happened. I guess I wanted her to think I was cool, and I guess I don't really think I'm cool normally. I mess up a lot and get in trouble a lot and the coolest thing about me is that

I draw, but Ellie makes movies, which is way more awesome.

I was really floundering my way through the conversation with Ellie, so it was a good thing when we were joined by others in the Young Artist program.

I got to meet everyone practically all at once, while our teachers all chatted, too. And I don't know about you, but I'm not so good with names. So to help you out, I've made a useful chart!

Introducing...EVERYONE!

Glen Coe
(poetry)

Thiago DaSilva
(collage)

Yrsa Jonsdottir
(music)

Eric Oka
(textile

Denny Bridges
(digital)

Monique Pham
(ceramics)

Vloot Van Vlader
(sculpture)

Linda Rubebi
(origami)

And of course, there was me and Ellie:

**Ellie Watts
(film/video)**

**Rafe
Khatchadorian
(illustration)**

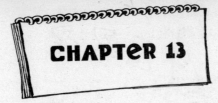

CHAPTER 13

BUNKING WITH A BULLDOZER

Bigbottom Creek might not have been the best-looking town in the country, but it knew how to make us feel welcome. Since all of us Young Artists were so hyped about the trip, we felt like friends already. Which was great, because the guys (me, Glen, Thiago, Vloot, Denny, and Eric) were sharing a room. This—like Ellie being here—had some good points and some bad ones.

Like I said, we were all friends so that was good.

The bad part was that when we went to bed, Thiago sounded like he was in training for the American Snoring Championships.

He fell asleep before I'd even put on my PJs! Me, I couldn't sleep. So I ended up staying awake thinking about the conversation I had with Mom earlier. I'd had to stand on my bed to get any reception. It was ridiculous!

"Hi, Mom," I'd said.

"Rafe! How's it going? How was the trip? How's the hotel? Did you have a good dinner? Have you made any friends yet?"

"Okay, okay." I laughed. "One question at a time! The trip was fine. Ellie, my friend from Australia, is here, so that's great! The hotel is…fine…" I decided right then and there that I wasn't going to tell my mom any of the bad parts about this trip. Not yet. I didn't want her to be upset that I was so excited to visit Hollywood and now it wasn't happening. And then she started asking all about Ellie, so I told her about that, and about meeting all the other Young Artists. Then she said she had to go to bed because it was late (time zones, remember?), even though I could tell she wanted to keep talking.

Thiago was still snoring, but I decided I didn't care anymore. One noisy kid wasn't going to get between me and ten hours of beautiful, uninterrupted shut-eye. I fell asleep to what sounded like a bulldozer stomping out a salsa beat from Thiago's bed.

Five seconds after my head touched the pillow, I was being shaken awake by a zombie.

Now was probably when I should've started running. That's how we're going to survive the Zombie Apocalypse, you know—running. Zombies aren't very fast.

But I was too tired.

If this is how I go, so be it!

Getting eaten by a zombie wasn't the *worst* way to go. It would make a pretty exciting story.

"Time to go, bud," the zombie said.

I blinked. The zombie looked back at me. It didn't seem to be trying to eat my brains…A closer look told me this wasn't a zombie at all. It was Denny.

I glanced through the window, at the black sky.

"You've got to be kidding me," I said. "It's still nighttime."

"Tell me about it," Denny said, his eyes half closed as he got dressed.

Ten minutes later, I was eating breakfast in a freezing-cold dining room with the rest of the Young Artists. It was four o'clock in the morning and the dining room at the Bigbottom Creek Hotel looked exactly how I imagine the world would look after a nuclear war.

"Can you believe this?" Ellie said.

I glanced up from my bowl of cereal. "Can't talk. Too early."

Which was a good excuse because the real reason I couldn't talk was that I kept thinking about how I kind of had a crush on her now. Was that weird? She was my friend—I couldn't have a crush on her!

Eric, who was sitting next to us, wore the disappointed expression of someone who'd been given crummy information about California being hot. He was wearing every item of clothing he'd brought with him.

"S-so c-cold," he said, his teeth chattering. He stared at me like everything was my fault.

Monique was in pretty much the same state as Eric, along with Glen, Linda, and Yrsa. Denny had his face flat on the table with drool pooling around his open mouth.

Even our teachers who'd come with us on the trip looked like icicles.

"It's a long drive out to the Rocky Hills," Brushes said, shouting over the clatter of dishes and cutlery. "Eat up, campers, and let's get this road on the show!"

I have a thing about people who say things like that. It's bad enough in the middle of the day.

At four in the morning it makes me want to put my head down on the table and cry. Still, I thought, things can only get better!

CHAPTER 14

THE LONGEST BUS RIDE OF MY LIFE

Things didn't get better.

After breakfast, we were all herded onto a bus. This one was different from the one that drove us here. That one was a normal bus, but this one kind of looked like a cattle truck with seats.

Hard balls of dried cow dung rolled around the floor. In a couple of places I could see the dirt road through rips in the rusty metal. In one corner of the roof was a bird's nest. All our gear, and all the gear for the camp, had been strapped to the top and sides.

Everyone found a spot and went to sleep, while up front, Brushes and his giant cousin, Vern, took turns driving. That's right: this drive was going to be so long it took *two* drivers to handle it. Woohoo!

Soon after we rolled out of Bigbottom Creek, the sun came up and I opened my eyes. They felt like they'd been taken out in the night, dipped in grit, and then replaced.

Still, the sunrise was awesome.

Maybe because we were surrounded by all that nothingness, the sun seemed to be about three times bigger than it was back in Hills Village, where it had to compete with things like trees and hills and strip malls and gas stations.

I fidgeted uncomfortably on the bone-hard seat and closed my eyes.

I was thinking about Jeanne Galletta, who

used to be the girl of my dreams until she made it clear we were JUST FRIENDS. So anyway, I was daydreaming about her and Ellie and what would happen if the two of them were in the same room— when someone tapped me on the shoulder.

I flinched, then opened my eyes. There was Ellie, and I looked around for Jeanne before remembering she wasn't here. And she and I were *just friends*. So were Ellie and I.

I mean, right?

My face got all hot again.

"How are you doing?" Ellie asked.

I nearly jumped out of my seat. What if she KNEW? Could she read it on my face? She could, couldn't she? She knew exactly what I'd been thinking and—

"I was doing okay till you woke me up," I said in a croaky voice, which is not the nicest way to talk to someone.

I don't even know why I said that. But I was worried Ellie had realized I maybe, kind of had a teensy tiny little crush on her…

Yes, I said it: CRUSH. I had a crush on Ellie.

Me being rude seemed to have canceled out any

possibility that she noticed, though. She gave me a look and left me alone, which was exactly the opposite of what I wanted.

The bus went over a particularly nasty bump and I almost hit the roof. If I hadn't already gotten used to the road I'd have bitten my tongue clean off.

"Whoa," Denny said, jerking awake. "Intense." He stretched and yawned.

"Dangerous, you mean," I said.

He laughed, then said, "So where are you from, Rafe?" He'd asked me exactly the same thing last night but must have forgotten.

I told him and he nodded, saying "Oh, cool," like he didn't already know.

"What about you?" he asked Ellie.

"Australia, mate!" she said.

"Whoa."

Suddenly, a bunch of other kids crowded around, because being from another country was capital C *cool*.

"So," Denny said, "do you guys, like, live in a hut or something?"

"Oh, of course," Ellie said. "Walk everywhere barefoot. Live off the land in the desert. Eat witchetty grubs and snakes, the odd lizard. Drink from ancient springs buried deep in the ground. Sleep in the day, walk at night."

I squinted at Ellie. I didn't remember her living like that when I visited…And I think I'd remember if she was someone who walked miles across a baking hot desert, but what did I know? I was from Hills Village. The nearest I ever got to a desert hike was getting caught in the Sahara Sand Trap during a round of putt-putt.

"I used some phozzies to see where I was going," Ellie went on.

"Phozzies?" Denny asked.

"Oh, I remember that from when I visited Australia!" I chimed in before Ellie could. "Those're giant phosphorescent bush moths *this* big." I spread my arms wide. "You get a couple of those guys and tie a string to their knees."

"Better 'n a Bunnings torch every time," Ellie said with a grin.

I beamed. I felt like I was about to float away because I'd *definitely* managed to impress Ellie. Then I realized:

She was giggling.

At *me*.

"What?" Did I have something on my face?

"Rafe," she said, trying to be serious. She kept giggling, though. "I told you that story. But it's not true. I made it up. I didn't realize…" She doubled over, laughing. "I didn't realize you fell for it."

"Wh-what?"

"I thought you knew it was a *joke*," she said, wiping away tears. "But nope. I got you—hook, line, *and* sinker." She hooked a finger inside her mouth and imitated a fish being caught.

"It's not funny," I said in a voice that meant I thought it was the opposite of funny.

"Yes, it is!" Ellie wheezed, holding her sides. "You seriously thought moths had *knees*?"

I turned my back to her and slithered down in my seat. So much for my stupid crush. She probably thought I was a total dweeb now.

CHAPTER 15

READY TO BE FLIPPED

I didn't sulk for too long—maybe two hours, three tops.

And all that time, the sun got a whole lot hotter. Remember how cold I said it was back at breakfast? We could only *wish* for that! Now it was hotter than the inside of Swifty's grill. If I was a burger, I'd be done.

"You folks okay in the back?" Brushes shouted. I tried to answer but my tongue was too dry. We were *cooking*. So much for our icicle teachers—now they were puddles. And I was pretty sure Glen had died or at least fallen into a coma. He hadn't made a sound since we'd set out. Hadn't these people heard of air-conditioning?

Sure, the windows of the bus were open, but all

that meant was that the thermonuclear desert air streaming in baked us just that little bit quicker. Before we were halfway to Rocky Hills, you could have fried eggs on my head.

The only good thing about the marathon drive was: (a) it was a long way from boring old Hills Village, and (b) we had plenty of time to get to know all the other Young Artists better.

I also had a long time to sit next to Ellie and try not to make a bigger fool of myself.

Denny helped out for a little while by talking. He sat behind us and chatted for a solid thirty minutes. He was next to Thiago, who'd apparently gotten tired of Denny's rambling. Denny told us all about his school (it sounded just as bad as Hills Village Middle School), his family (they *didn't* sound as great as mine), and his hobbies (which mostly sounded boring, except for one in particular). Denny was super into digital stuff, and that included HACKING.

Yup, he bragged all about how he'd hacked into different sites and was planning to make it big one day. I didn't exactly believe him. I was pretty sure he was just trying to impress Ellie, which put me in a worse mood.

After Denny ran out of things to talk about—I thought it might never happen!—I pulled out my sketchbook. I started to draw me and Ellie, out in the hot desert, alone. We're walking through the burning sand when up ahead we see this *huge* resort, complete with an in-ground pool, a waterslide, and ice-cold soda.

It definitely wasn't there before and I'm not sure how we didn't notice it until now, but who cares! Ellie and I run for it—

But it keeps staying in the same place, just out of reach.

"No!" I say.

That's when the sand shoots up in front of us, like a tidal wave. "Not so fast!" it says, shifting into a hundred-foot-tall sand monster. "You've got to get past *me* first!"

"How's it going?" Mrs. Donatello asks, materializing next to me and Ellie.

"Um, really?" I point at the *monster* towering over us. "Not so great!"

"Rafe?"

I blinked and I was back on the bus. Mrs. Donatello had twisted around in her seat and was looking at me. I hoped she hadn't heard me embarrassing myself in front of Ellie.

"You doing okay?" Mrs. Donatello asked.

"Fine," I said. "Just bored."

"Yes, it is a long drive," she said.

"Yeah. It's also kind of hard to draw while moving," I said.

"Still looks pretty good," Ellie said, peering over my shoulder. "Is that—?"

"Nope." I quickly shut my sketchbook.

"I swear it looked like me—"

"NOPE!" I stood, and nearly fell back down

again when we hit a huge bump. "How much longer?" I called to Brushes.

"Sit yer butt back down and hold yer horses!" he said.

I imagined jumping out the window. I'd probably break an arm or a leg, but it might be the only way I'd stop embarrassing myself in front of Ellie.

CHAPTER 16

THE GREAT BIG NOTHING

All bad things come to an end eventually—but I bet the person who came up with that saying never took a bus ride from Bigbottom Creek to the middle of nowhere, while sitting next to his crush who he made a fool of himself in front of.

By the time we got where we were going, I'd started thinking we'd entered some sort of desert Bermuda Triangle and were going to be stuck in a never-ending bus ride *forever*.

So long, Mom! So long, Georgia, Grandma Dotty, and Junior! It was nice knowing ya!

But finally—FINALLY—we reached our destination. Which was...

Nothing.

Yup. I don't even know if Vern was actually driving to this spot specifically, or if he just gave up and parked the bus somewhere. This part of the desert looked exactly like every other part we'd passed.

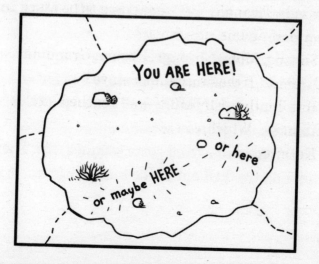

There was scrub, a few rocks with a bigger heap of rocks in the distance, and then a great big heap of nothing. The nothingness stretched toward the horizon in all directions. It was the most nothing I had ever seen in one place.

What *had* I been expecting? Guitar-shaped swimming pools? Shopping malls? The Taj Mahal?

Actually, I'd been expecting movie stars and the red carpet and palm trees and paparazzi. But, well...After *that* I'd just thought wherever we were going would have, I dunno, a *hint* of civilization. An outhouse or porta-potty. A tent or two. *Something*.

"Okay, folks, look lively!" Brushes said, sounding way too cheerful for someone who'd just gone through what we'd gone through. "We've got a camp to set up!"

I tried to stand, but after bouncing around in the back of the sun-temperature bus for about a century, all feeling had gone out of the Khatchadorian *gluteus maximus*.

Everyone else looked sorta stunned, too. They got up and trekked out of the bus in a daze, including our teachers. Finally, I stepped outside and it was hotter out there than a Mexican chile with extra chile on the side.

Remember when I said there was *camping* involved? Well, that's what happened next! And none of us were exactly happy about it.

Once we got off the bus, we all sort of just stood there. I bet Mrs. Donatello was regretting being my chaperone.

"All right, Cultural Campers, find a spot," Brushes said, smiling. At least, I think he was smiling. It was hard to tell behind all that face fungus.

"Where's the campsite?" I asked.

"You're standing on the campsite, Ralphie, my man," he said.

We stared at him.

"I thought this was an *art* camp," Thiago said.

"Exactly!" Brushes said. "You're artists, and we're camping."

I groaned.

"Worst surprise ever," Ellie whispered to me.

It was like we'd arrived on the dark side of the moon. A lizard about the size of a Labrador scuttled past and gave us a long disgusted stare before disappearing under a rock.

"This is *really* the camp?" Vloot asked.

"Looks that way," Ellie said. With her foot, she prodded her sleeping bag, which Brushes had unloaded from the bus. "And this is what we're sleeping on."

"What about tents?" Glen said.

"Y'know," Denny said, "this is just like the start of a horror movie, when a bunch of kids go somewhere real far from everything and then at night they start disappearing and stuff."

"I'm scared," Linda said in a small voice.

"He's making things up," Ellie said to her. "We're all going to be fine."

A weird dragging sound was coming from somewhere behind me. I turned to see Cousin Vern pulling an axe out of a metal toolbox, and I jumped about eight feet in the air.

Vern lumbers toward us, axe gripped in both hands, and this totally murderous look in his eyes. One of us is definitely not making it home alive— but I'm not letting that happen!

I'm going to be a *hero*!

I brandish a lightsaber and step in front of Ellie and everyone else (but mostly Ellie—I really need to impress her and make up for being an idiot before).

"Hey," Vern says, nodding at his axe and then my lightsaber. "No fair!"

"Yes, it is!" I say. "I'm the hero."

Vern growls, raising his axe. There's blood on it. He swings for my head—

I lift my lightsaber, cutting the axe in half. The sharp part falls onto the sand. Now Vern just has a stumpy stick.

He's weaponless! Now for the killing blow!

Except, I don't want to kill him. Just knock him out.

I grab a rock off the ground.

Now, normally I'm not the most athletic kid. But right now, I'm in charge of saving all my new friends—and making a good impression on Ellie. So I throw the rock.

The rock hits Vern right between the eyes. It splits in two as Vern topples over, landing flat on his back next to the destroyed axe.

Everybody is cheering as the other adults remove the axe pieces and the unconscious Vern. Denny claps me on the shoulder and says, "That was amazing, man!"

"You saved us!" Monique cries.

"My hero!" Ellie says, and then she sweeps me off my feet and kisses me.

"Rafe? Yo! *Rafe*."

I jumped out of my skin.

Okay, not literally. But almost.

I realized I'd been daydreaming again, and Ellie was standing next to me.

The kiss wasn't real, but the red-hot blush on my face sure was.

"Don't look so scared, Rafe," she said. "He's not *actually* going to murder us."

"Yeah—yeah I know," I said, but I wasn't sure Ellie bought it.

Today was going *awesome*.

And that's sarcasm. I actually couldn't imagine how it could go any worse.

Of course, that's when the universe decided to show me exactly how bad things could get.

CHAPTER 17

FAMOUS LAST WORDS

I was so embarrassed I couldn't look at Ellie as we arranged our bags around the spot where Brushes was going to start a campfire. He had us all drag some big rocks closer, too. It wasn't exactly the Ritz but it was more comfortable than you might think. While we were doing that, Cousin Vern started to make dinner.

This was good and bad.

On the one hand, I *was* starving. On the other, it meant Vern had swapped his axe for a large knife.

Brushes got the fire going and, in about three seconds, it was burning away like he'd flicked an ON switch. Remember how hot it had been? Well, now with the sun dipping below the horizon, the temperature was starting to drop pretty quick.

As the sun disappeared, Brushes called us over to get some food. And you know what? Vern had done a pretty good job on the barbecue. He'd even catered to the two vegetarians in the group.

Okay, so he hadn't exactly gone to a lot of trouble by throwing six veggie sausages on the griddle, but I guess the thought was there. I was so hungry I could have eaten a slice of fried tire and a side of sand, but sinking my teeth into the sausage slathered in ketchup was a whole lot better.

We sat on our rocks around the fire and ate and talked.

It was good.

With some food in my belly, my new friends to hang out with, and the campfire burning away, I started warming up to Camp Culture again. Maybe I'd misjudged Brushes and Vern. They might *look* like weirdo serial killers, but they had set up a pretty cool campsite and made a good dinner. I guess it wasn't their fault I'd thought California meant Hollywood. (Though, who can blame me?)

I leaned back against my rock, listened to the fire crackling, and looked up at the stars. I could feel the magic of the wilderness settling into my soul.

Maybe this wasn't so bad.

Maybe the peace and quiet of nature was exactly what I needed.

Maybe—

That's when Brushes grabbed a box from the bus and bellowed, "Who needs to poop?!"

CHAPTER 18

KHATCHADORIAN -1

I should've kept my big mouth shut. But I couldn't help it.

First of all, there was just something about McGarrity's bristly leather face that made me want to show him we weren't total dorks.

But second of all—and most important—I was in desperate need of a way to impress Ellie. I had to make up for not one, but *two* times I'd made a fool of myself. So when Brushes pulled out the spade, I jumped right in.

"I know what those are," I shouted as Brushes took tiny shovels out of the box. "It's a poop spade. For burying our poop, right?"

Chalk one up to me: Khatchadorian 1, McGarrity 0!

Also, bonus points for impressing Ellie.

Right?

I turned to Ellie, expecting to see her looking wowed. Instead, she looked grossed out.

"Do you usually go around shoveling your own poop?" Ellie asked.

Khatchadorian -1.

I sunk into my seat, wishing I could disappear.

"Ralph's right," Brushes announced.

"What?" Vloot gasped. "There're no toilets? Is that even *legal*?"

Denny took the spade from Brushes and gave it a look so full of disgust I was surprised the thing didn't melt. "That is *so* not cool."

Thiago laughed as if he'd never heard anything so ridiculous. Linda put her hand to her mouth and looked like she was going to be sick.

I know what you're all thinking (besides wondering why I'm such an idiot and keep making a fool of myself in front of Ellie): when did Rafe Khatchadorian get so wise and stuff about wilderness toilets? Huh? And I'd say to you: the Program.

On the Program at Camp Wannamorra, I'd

dealt with a lot more than pooping in the woods. I'd taken everything Sergeant Fish had thrown at me with a smile on my face. Okay, maybe I didn't actually smile *all* the time, but you know what I mean. I'd done some wild camping, I'd survived raging rivers, and I'd faced down bears. How bad could it be at Camp Culture? Being a Man of Experience was something I was getting to like. I could almost feel my brain absorbing the idea that things that seem unpleasant at the time can, in the end, make you a stronger person.

But then Ellie scooted her rock a few inches away from me, and my spirits fell.

To make things *even worse,* that's when Brushes started singing.

And trust me—until you've heard Brushes McGarrity "singing" "The Man from Snowy River," you haven't truly suffered. But he didn't stop there. Wilderness stories, poetry, and the tale of his discovery of the cave paintings came next. The man just went on and on.

And on. And on.

To be fair, some of what Brushes was saying was *kind of* interesting. And he sure looked the part.

He was wearing a cowboy hat and a battered jacket made out of what looked like (and probably was) an old tarp off the back of a truck. Lit by the flickering campfire, he could have stepped straight out of 1892.

"Mysterious place, eh?" he said, holding his hands out to the flames. He stared at each of us. "It's been a sacred place for generations. There're also legends of mythical animals out here, so don't be surprised if you spot creatures out here tonight."

Denny snorted, then quickly covered it up with a cough when Brushes glared at him. "Got a bit of sausage stuck in there," Denny said, pointing at his throat.

"You need to watch that," Brushes growled, standing up. "Could be dangerous." He gave Denny a meaningful glare. "Best make it an early one tonight, campers. We'll be heading to the Rocky Hills tomorrow to see my famous McGarrity Cave Paintings—the finest cave paintings in the whole of California and you'll all want to be fresh for *that*." He jerked a thumb at the bus. "Vern's rigging up a shower over there for anyone who needs it."

"Starting with Vern," Ellie whispered.

I tried to come up with a great response, but all I could say was, "Uh-huh."

"Not enough water in all of Cali to get that dude clean," Denny said.

See, a response like *that*!

"Any questions?" Brushes asked.

Vloot put up a hand. "Hot tub?"

"The wilderness's no place for softies," Brushes said. His smile was still in place but his eyes narrowed. It wasn't something to get worked up about, but I could tell Brushes McGarrity wasn't someone who liked to be the butt of anyone's joke.

As if to confirm this, he scratched his beard in a way that seemed to be saying, "I'm onto you, Vloot." He pulled down the brim of his hat so all I could see of his eyes were two pinpricks of reflected light. Vloot looked like he'd seen a ghost.

He paused and pointed a finger at the group, his voice going even lower and growlier than it had been before. It was the voice of the guy who does the voice-overs on scary movie trailers. "G'night, campers. Sleep tight. Hope the snakes don't bite."

"*Snakes?*" Monique yelped.

Brushes turned and walked off into the darkness. There was no sign of Vern.

Even after the fire had gone out and all the other campers were fast asleep, I was wide awake. Maybe it was jet lag. Maybe it was the sausages gurgling in my stomach. Or maybe, just maybe, it was the thought of being bitten in my sleep by a snake.

Was I the ONLY sane one here?

Wasn't anyone else even a *little* concerned about whatever was roaming around in the desert? And were Brushes and Vern supposed to just abandon us like that? I mean, sure, our teachers were here, but I didn't think Mrs. Donatello would be much help against a venomous snake.

I tried counting sheep but they kept getting eaten by giant snakes, swallowed whole. Plus, every time I was about to drift off, I'd hear a squeak or a rustle, and my head would pop back up, my eyes wide, hopelessly scanning the blackness for whatever was out there.

It was going to be a long night.

CHAPTER 19

BAAAAAAAAAAAAAACON!

Wakey, wakey! Rise and shine, campers!"
Brushes shouted.

Behind him, Vern was making so much noise cooking that Brushes had to shout louder than he normally did, which meant he was about as loud as a fighter-jet engine.

One by one, the bleary-eyed campers and art teachers staggered to their feet.

"Today's the day you lucky, lucky people get to see the McGarrity Cave Paintings: the best cave paintings in the whole of California!" Brushes continued.

An incredible smell of bacon wafted over from where Vern was cooking.

Baaaaaaaaaaaaaaaaaaaaaacon!

Despite how tired I was, that stuff smelled
good, but then you'd have to be in a coma not to
love the smell of bacon in the morning. I wondered
if the vegetarians in our group felt the same way.
Probably not.

About an hour after waking up we were all
aboard the bus, clutching our various bits of art
gear, and the events of the previous day began to
fade—the long trip out here, the uncomfortable
sleeping situation...

I took a large sketchbook and some pastels. A
couple of the others—Vloot and Thiago—did the

same while Linda hauled out a thick wad of paper. Ellie had her trusty video camera around her neck. Denny took a remote satellite transmitter and laptop and was planning to live-blog the whole thing right from the caves.

Yrsa had a violin and a neat digital recorder—she was going to tape the noises inside the caves and use them in a musical composition. Monique had a special "toolbox" with a ton of empty drawers she was going to fill with colored dirt, leaves, bits of rock, and anything else she could use in her ceramics.

Eric carried a huge bag of wool. I had no idea what he was planning but he looked like he knew what he was doing. Glen had the least to carry: just a chewed-up pencil and a battered black notebook.

Suddenly, I realized something—*this* was why I was here.

These were the kinds of people I wanted to be around. It was all cool. It was all fun. I felt like a real art student.

I felt like I belonged.

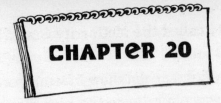

CHAPTER 20

WELCOME TO MCGARRITYLAND

Up ahead, a red hill stuck straight out of the flat desert like a pimple. Brushes pulled the bus off the road and we bumped along a winding track through a bunch of weird-looking boulders.

"There she blows," Brushes shouted. He pointed out the window at a sharp black slice cut into the big red rock. "The McGarrity Caves!"

"Are they called the McGarrity Caves?" I asked. "Officially, I mean."

"That's what *he* calls them," Denny said. "But I'm sure they were called something else before Brushes came along."

"This place used to be part of tribal lands," Ellie said. "I read about it online. The caves belonged to the local Native Americans, not people like McGarrity who swoop in out of nowhere."

"I don't understand," I said. "Why aren't the cave paintings named after *them*?"

"Good question," she said. "They're long gone from around here. They were run off when settlers found valuables in the ground."

"There's gold here?"

Ellie shrugged. "Not sure. What I read didn't say exactly what was mined, but, whatever it was, it all ran out long ago," she said. "Too late for the locals even if they did come back."

"It could've been diamonds!" I said excitedly.

"There aren't any diamond mines in California," Ellie pointed out.

And immediately I felt stupid. I looked away so she didn't see me turning red.

"You probably just have diamonds on the brain," she added, "from hearing about that big ol' blue one that went missing."

"Oh, the Brilliant Bluebird Diamond?" Vloot chimed in. "I heard about that, too!"

"Yeah," I muttered, "probably just that."

As I sunk down in my seat—trying to come up with ways to stop looking like an idiot in front of Ellie—I noticed Brushes eyeing us through the rearview mirror. There was a weird look in his eye...then it was gone, and he said, "We're here!"

Brushes pulled the bus to a stop outside the cave entrance.

CHAPTER 21

RAFE KHATCHADORIAN, SPELUNCAPHOBIC

Okay, so remember how I wasn't thrilled about camping?

I was even *less* thrilled about going into a cave. This was going to be…not fun.

Why couldn't we just keep doing art above ground? I know the whole point of this trip was to see cave paintings, but did we *really* need to see them? Couldn't we just look the images up online, from our nice, warm, safe homes? That sounded like a MUCH better plan.

"Once you get belowground," McGarrity warned us, "the temperature drops right quick, make no mistake. Better put on your jackets. Now, is everyone ready to see the best cave art in the whole of California?"

I swallowed hard. I wanted to say no, but that would make me look even more pathetic in front of Ellie...

I'd been trying not to worry about this ever since I found out we'd be visiting the paintings, but...I couldn't ignore it anymore.

I *really* don't like caves.

Don't get me wrong. I'm not claustrophobic. I'm fine in elevators or closets or whatever. No, it's real specific. There's even a name for it. I mean, I don't freak out or start screaming or anything, but as we approached the narrow gap in the rock wall, I felt a cold globule of fear trickle down my spine.

Close up, the cave looked about as inviting as a shark's mouth, and I wasn't about to accept that invitation.

What if the whole thing collapsed on us? What if we got trapped inside?

What if I got lost in there and spent the rest of my life looking for the way out by feeling my way

through inky blackness until my strength gave out and I tried to climb the walls but slipped and got wedged upside down in a crevasse, screaming and screaming but there's no one there?

Okay, maybe I'm getting carried away, but on the news there's always some guy getting trapped upside down in a cave.

They *always* get trapped upside down, too. No idea why, it's just what happens. *I* didn't want to be trapped upside down in a cave. I didn't even want to be *in* the cave. But there was no going back now, not unless I wanted to look like a total coward in front of Ellie and the rest of them.

Not. An. Option.

CHAPTER 22

BLOOD CAVES 3: REVENGE OF THE GHOST CAVE

Brushes stopped in front of the cave entrance and gathered us around in a semicircle.

"Okay, guys and gals, this first part is a bit of a doozy. But I think youse'll all be *fine*."

Ellie leaned over to me and whispered, "Famous last words? Or you reckon we'll be okay?"

I was so happy Ellie was talking to me that my brain stopped working and all I said in response was, "Uh."

"Now," Brushes said, while waving to Vern to come closer, "you're going to need these."

Vern opened the large bag he was carrying and handed us orange hard hats with LED flashlights attached. We put them on and I looked around at the group, laughing and taking photos of one another. I guessed no one else was speluncaphobic. I wished our teachers would decide this was too dangerous for us, but they didn't say anything. Guess they trusted Vern and Brushes to know what they were doing. Me? I didn't.

"Cheer up," Ellie said. "You look like you've seen a ghost."

I did that thing with your mouth where you smile but the person looking at you knows you're not really smiling. And the reason was that Ellie was almost right. I hadn't seen a ghost but I'd watched this scene before—a bunch of laughing kids heading into a cave—and I knew exactly how it ended. It was a late-night flick I'd secretly watched on my computer about six months back and immediately regretted.

The McGarrity Caves looked exactly like the cave in *Blood Caves 3*.

And we were going in.

We followed Brushes to the cave entrance with Vern waving as we went. He was too big to fit through the entrance. Lucky Vern.

Brushes went in first, turning sideways and disappearing into the darkness, his LED light flickering across the cave walls. The rest of the group went in one by one while I hung back.

It wasn't until everyone was almost inside that I realized I'd forgotten something Very Important.

I couldn't be the last in line. No freakin' way!

Everyone *knows* that in any horror movie the

kid at the end of the line is the one who dies first.
It doesn't matter where they are—in the jungle,
haunted house, abandoned fairground, whatever—
they're a sure-fire goner.

It was right up there with volunteering to go
outside to check what that weird noise was, or
suggesting everyone splits up, or putting your face
right up close to a darkened window…all things
that, in the movies, meant you were first on the
chopping block.

Rule #1: Don't be last in line

I sprinted forward, and slid sideways into the cave. I had to elbow Monique out of the way, which I kind of felt bad about—honest!—but not bad enough to stop me from doing it...

I'd apologize later. *If* we survived.

CHAPTER 23

THE TRICKY PART

The inside of the cave wasn't as bad as I'd thought it would be.

It was much, much, *much* worse.

For one thing, it was way darker. It was like being the filling in some giant sandwich. The light from the flashlight kept bouncing back into my eyes off the rock wall, which meant that I was pretty much blind. My heart was beating real quick and my breathing was shallow. I sounded like an asthmatic poodle. I'd only taken about three steps and I already felt trapped. What was it going to be like farther in?

I tried to be braver, or at least act braver (which, I've noticed, are pretty much the same thing), and inched along. I shuffled sideways, the rock walls getting closer and closer until it seemed impossible to go any farther.

"Okay, people," Brushes called from up ahead, "this is the tricky part."

I'd thought for sure we were already in the "tricky part." How could this nightmare possibly get any worse?

"Everyone drop to the ground and crawl," Brushes instructed. "The ceiling gets pretty low around here."

Okay, that's how it could get worse.

Now I was regretting letting Monique go last. It meant I couldn't get out even if I wanted to—not unless Monique went with me, and even I wasn't going to be that much of a coward.

Not with Ellie there. I dropped to the ground and started crawling.

The cave seemed to shrink to nothing and the tops of our helmets began to scrape against the roof as we crawled forward. I could feel the ground sloping away and I had to dig in with my elbows to stop from sliding.

Directly ahead of me, the soles of Eric's feet scrabbled along the tunnel floor. Everyone was very quiet as we crawled and crawled and crawled for what seemed like forever.

It wasn't funny anymore.

I was going to die in here. This was it for Rafe Khatchadorian. RIP me.

I might not be dangling upside down but I knew that we were all going to get wedged in this impossibly narrow cave tunnel and...

Just like that, we popped out of the tunnel onto the ground. I landed facedown in a patch of dust and began sneezing.

"Wow," I heard Ellie say.

I sneezed one last time and looked up.

Wow is right.

CHAPTER 24

DOUBLE AWESOME WITH SPRINKLES ON TOP

Not too shabby, eh?" Brushes said. He spread his arms out wide. There was no mistaking his pride. It was like he owned the place. Maybe he did. I was a bit sketchy on the land ownership laws in the remote areas of California. Or anywhere, really. He was right, though. This place was not in any way shabby.

We stood at the base of a towering cavern dotted with pillars of sandstone that reached up to the cave roof, which glittered as our flashlight beams crisscrossed over it. It was double awesome with sprinkles on top. And strawberry sauce.

For a few seconds we all just stood and gaped.

"Gold?" Vloot said, pointing at the ceiling.

Brushes shook his head and smiled. "No, that's iron pyrite, better known as fool's gold. Looks pretty, eh? But totally worthless." He turned and walked across the cavern. "This way."

"Isn't this awesome?" Ellie whispered to me.

I nodded, and I'm glad I could pretend I was speechless because of the cave.

(Three guesses why I was *really* speechless.)

Brushes stopped at the far wall of the cavern.

He took a lantern from his pack and switched it on. "Can you all turn your head lights off?" he said. "These cave paintings are light-sensitive."

We did as he asked and the cavern was bathed in a soft, warm glow. Brushes walked the lantern a few paces to his left and placed it on the floor.

"Behold the McGarrity Paintings!" Brushes stood back as the lantern lit up the cavern wall.

The cavern wall was absolutely full of paintings and patterns drawn and scratched into the surface. It was easy to make out images of various animals. There were some symbols in there—things I couldn't recognize. It was amazing.

"It all looks so fresh!" Ellie said.

Brushes nodded. "That's the atmospheric pressure down here. It's great for preserving everything just as they were twenty thousand years ago."

"Twenty *thousand* years?" I said.

Beside me there was a chorus of *ooh*s and *aah*s. People took out their cameras and sketchbooks, and Brushes kept up a commentary on the paintings while we got busy.

I began to wonder if I had been too hard on old Brushes. The cave paintings *were* totally awesome.

Twenty thousand years! Even Grandma Dotty wouldn't remember that far back.

(If you're reading this, GD, I'm only joking!)

"You've got about thirty minutes," Brushes said. "Just being here can affect the pigments in the paintings. Any longer and we risk destroying them with the carbon dioxide in our breath. That's why I need you all to stay well back."

We settled in and did our thing.

But after about twenty minutes, I noticed Ellie moving closer and closer to the wall. She seemed real interested in a painting of some kind of antelope. When she was about an arm's length from the cave wall, I saw her frown.

"HEY!" Brushes yelled, his voice echoing off the cavern walls, making about half of us drop our pencils. "Get back!"

Ellie just looked at him, then slowly walked back over to the rest of us.

"Let's go!" Brushes yelled. "Right now!" He began making shooing motions like we were a herd of badly behaved sheep. "There's always one who ruins things for everyone else! Pack up your stuff, we're heading back to camp!"

CHAPTER 25

SNIFFING ANTELOPE BUTT

Nice going, Ellie," Denny said, knocking her with his shoulder as he passed.

To be honest, leaving the cavern was sort of okay with me. I mean, the paintings were triple-super-cool and all but we were still in *Blood Caves 3*. We packed up our stuff and walked back to the crawl tunnel.

With one last angry glance at Ellie—who didn't seem to care at all—Brushes scrambled up.

"Everyone follow me," he said, and headed into the tunnel. "Move it!" His feet disappeared and, one by one, the rest of the group slipped in behind him.

In a couple of minutes it was my turn. As I started climbing, I felt a hand on my arm.

It was Ellie.

She put a finger to her lips and motioned for me to follow her, dragging me away from the mouth of the tunnel.

"What are you doing?" I shook my head and stopped dead. Ellie was great and all, but no *way* was I separating from the group with her. I mean, not while we were in a CAVE.

"Come," she said, and began pulling me back to the cave paintings.

I glanced at the tunnel. Everyone else had gone. Ellie kept tugging my arm.

"Please, Rafe?" She gave me an evil look. "Or are you too *scared*?"

Me, Rafe Khatchadorian, SCARED?

Ha!

But for real? I was actually very scared. Except I couldn't let Ellie know that, so I had to play it cool.

I could do cool—right?

"Well?" Ellie asked. "You coming?"

"Yeah, of course I'm coming," I said.

But I was thinking, *Be cool, be cool, be cool.*

We ran across the empty cavern to the cave paintings. With everyone else gone, the place seemed even bigger and way spookier.

"This is *so* bad," I said.

My mom had specifically said not to get into any trouble, and this sure felt like the beginning of trouble.

"See," Ellie said, beckoning me over to the antelope drawing.

"What?" Close up, the drawing looked even better but I still couldn't see why she was getting so worked up. I shrugged. "I don't get it."

Ellie rolled her eyes and pointed to her nose and then at the antelope's butt. "Go on. Smell it."

I bent my head to the antelope's butt and sniffed.

CHAPTER 26

SPILL THE BEANS

What kept you two so long?" Brushes glared at Ellie and me as we wriggled out of the cave, blinking against the glare of the sun. "Not up to any *funny business,* were you?"

My face went red, red, RED.

"I got stuck in the tunnel," Ellie said, saving both our butts by coming up with an excuse fast. "Rafe was behind me, so…"

Brushes eyed her, then me. I tried to look innocent, but I don't think I managed too well. I was glad I was all squinty, otherwise I'm pretty sure Brushes would have spotted how guilty I was right away. But thanks to the sun, he didn't notice.

But Mrs. Donatello, on the other hand…

"Rafe!" She stormed over. "What were you

doing? It's dangerous in there! You and Ellie could've been hurt!"

I felt like I was on trial.

I looked at the ground and mumbled. "I know. Sorry."

Mrs. Donatello softened. "Just be careful, okay?"

I nodded. After she walked away, Ellie winked at me. I almost died.

Once we were back on the bus, Denny said, "What was *that* all about?"

He, along with Ellie, Thiago, and I, were in the two back rows. It was even bumpier and smellier back there but it was as far away from the adults as we could get.

At the front of the bus, Brushes seemed to be concentrating on his driving, although I did see his eyes flick up to his rearview mirror more than a couple of times. I half-turned in my seat so he couldn't see my face.

"Ellie noticed something funny in the cavern," I whispered.

"What do you mean by 'funny'?" Denny asked.

I hesitated. Did I *really* want to get into all this? Mom didn't want me getting in any trouble, and so far, I'd been managing!

Surprising, I know.

But something weird was going on here, and I couldn't just sit back and let it happen. I mean, could I?

I was on an *adventure,* after all. This was my chance to do something really memorable!

(And not awful, like the nightmare feel of crawling into that cave.)

I was Rafe Khatchadorian, adventurer extraordinaire—and I wasn't passing this up. No way!

"Spill it!" Denny said.

"Okay," I said, leaning in closer. "Listen up."

Then Ellie and I explained everything.

CHAPTER 27

NO PLACE TO BE ENEMIES

I put on my ultra-serious face. "The antelope's butt smelled like paint."

"So?" Denny said. "What's wrong with a painting smelling like paint? I mean, it is a *paint*ing, right?"

I raised my eyebrows and waited for the lightbulb to go off. Sure enough, after a second or two, Denny's eyebrows shot up to match mine.

Meaningful eyebrow raise

"*Oh!*" Denny said, louder than I liked. "The painting shouldn't smell of paint—"

"Because it's supposed to be twenty thousand years old," Ellie said, completing Denny's thought.

"Exactly," I said, sitting back.

"*The paintings are fake!*" Denny hissed.

"Yep," Ellie said.

Denny was bouncing around in his seat and it wasn't just because we were driving across a dried-up creek bed. He slapped his hand on the back of my seat. "I *knew* there was something weird about that guy!"

I glanced at Ellie, who was sitting quite still. "What's up?"

"I don't know…" she said. "It's a pretty big thing to accuse Brushes of faking the paintings. Like, who says it was *him*?"

I nodded and said, "I'm not accusing Brushes. Not yet. Not until we've figured something out."

"What's that?" Denny said.

"*Why* he faked them," I said. He didn't seem to be making a ton of money from these campouts, and he certainly wasn't famous for finding the paintings.

"*If* he faked them," Ellie corrected. "We can't jump to conclusions."

"The place is named after him," I said. "He found the paintings and everything. How would he not know they're fake?"

"Maybe they were fading away and he was worried they'd disappear," Thiago suggested. "Still bad, I know, but different than faking the whole thing."

I opened my mouth to argue and then closed it again.

He was right. Brushes' crime might be vandalism, not forgery. There was a big difference.

I looked out of the bus window. That was the thing about the desert—there was plenty of space to hide things, plenty of space to get lost. We were a long way from home out here.

It was no place to be making enemies.

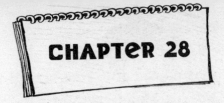

CHAPTER 28

REMEMBER THAT SCENE IN *JURASSIC PARK*?

That night, after getting back to the campsite from our traumatizing cave experience (okay, so maybe it was only traumatizing for *me*), we were all exhausted. But no matter how hard I tried, I couldn't sleep.

I kept noticing…things.

Like a sound that I *knew* wasn't in my imagination. My eyes snapped open. This wasn't an imaginary squeak. It was a very real *boofboom* kind of thing way off in the distance.

I'm pretty sure it was the type of sound some tourist-munching desert monster thing would make.

I sat bolt upright, every Khatchadorian nerve ending vibrating like crazy.

"H-he-llo?" I said. "Is anyone there?" (Like a monster would reply.)

GULP!

Boofboom.

There it was again, closer and louder this time and about fifty times more scary.

"D-d-did anyone else h-hear th-that?" I whispered, the words dry in my throat.

The only answer came in the form of a fart from somewhere over near Thiago. It was the one time in my life I've been glad to hear a fart. At least it meant everyone else wasn't already dead.

"Ellie? Denny?" I croaked. "Glen?" Not a peep.

Maybe under different circumstances I'd be glad Ellie didn't wake up and see me being such a baby, but right now? I didn't care.

BOOFBOOM!

Whatever was making that sound was getting *really* close to the campsite. I could feel the bass notes vibrating under my already twitchy butt. It was exactly like that dinosaur movie.

You know the one where the kids are trapped in the jeep just outside the T. rex enclosure and there's a glass of water (why?) on the dash?

Everything's real quiet and then the kid hears a sort of *boof* noise and the water ripples outward from the center of the glass and the kid knows—just *knows*—that the sound is caused by the massive thudding footsteps of...

AN ENORMOUS T. REX THAT'S GETTING NEARER AND NEARER AND—

CHAPTER 29

THE STINK FROM BEYOND THE BEYOND

*B*OOFBOOM!

The whole camp was shaking now.

Directly above my head—so close I could almost touch it—a massive shape as black as a school principal's heart hurtled across the star-spangled sky. I caught a brief flash of razor-sharp teeth, the red glint of a glowing evil eye, and then whatever the thing was landed on the other side of the camp with another colossal *BOOFBOOM!*

Trembling more than a bobblehead toy on the top of the Empire State Building in a hurricane, I listened to it thudding across the desert until there was just silence. And a smell.

Oh, man, *what* a smell!

This was a stench from beyond the grave: a stanky, stinky, stenchy reek-o-rama so completely and utterly 110 percent downright *nasty* that my nostrils begged for mercy.

It smelled worse than the dumpster behind Swifty's in a heat wave. Worse than the time I went to the bathroom straight after Miller the Killer had broken the school record for eating enchiladas. Worse than a vat of sixty-year-old rotten eggs and fish heads topped with a layer of used diapers.

Coughing, eyes stinging, heart pounding, I crawled to my bag and, with a trembling hand, took out my sketchbook.

By the time I finished the sketch, my heart rate had gone down to a manageable four zillion beats per minute. As I was wondering what to do next, Ellie woke up.

"What's going on?" she said in a sleep-thickened voice.

I decided to play things cool. Obviously.

For one thing, no one would believe for a second that a mutant, fart-powered giant crocodile had just bounced across the campsite. I'd look like a complete idiot if I said anything.

For another, this was *Ellie* we were talking about. I didn't want to look like an idiot in front of anyone, but I REALLY didn't want to look like an idiot in front of *her*.

So, like the cool, calm, and collected person I am, I said:

"Amutantfart-poweredgiantcrocodilejustbounced-acrossthecampsite!"

Oh, well.

But hey! In my defense, that playing it cool thing is always *way* harder than it seems. I know I'd lasted all of two nanoseconds, but *you* try doing better when you're freaked out *and* the girl you're crushing on is sitting right there!

"Look!" I said, and held out the sketch for Ellie to see. (And—before anyone gets all snarky about it being nighttime and all "how would anyone be able to see a sketchbook in the dark, huh?"—I was using my otherwise useless phone as a flashlight.)

"Nice drawing," Ellie mumbled, and lay back down.

"No! You don't understand! This thing was RIGHT HERE!"

Ellie yawned and pointed past my shoulder. "You mean like that one?"

I turned to see a giant mutant crocodile standing above me, its drooling jaws and glowing eyes illuminated by the light from my phone.

"Yes," I said, turning back to Ellie, "exactly like tha—"

The words froze in my throat. A thick spatter of giant crocodile drool hissed as it hit the dying embers of the fire. Directly above my head, the creature's jaws slowly opened. From my angle it seemed to be smiling. There was a moment's pause and then, faster than I would have believed possible, the crocodile lunged at me. I opened my mouth to scream but it was too late…

And no, I know what you're thinking, but this wasn't one of my daydreams where my imagination runs wild and I make you think crazy stuff is happening.

This was *real*.

CHAPTER 30

WORSE THAN BEING EATEN BY A CROC

R afe! Rafe!" Ellie cried out in horror.

Oh, bummer, she was about to see me looking *really* uncool…

I tried to scramble out of my sleeping bag, but my foot got caught and I landed flat on my face.

Ow.

Then the crocodile was on top of me. It grabbed me with its teeth and tossed me around like a toy. I felt the creature's monstrous jaws clamp onto my arm and…

"RAFE!"

I opened my eyes, expecting to be staring down the throat of the giant mutant croc.

But nope. It was WORSE.

Ellie stood over me, shaking my arm.

And okay, I know what you're thinking. You're going, *Um, Rafe? How is that WORSE than getting eaten by a crocodile???*

I'll tell you how:

1. Because it was dark, no light from a phone.
2. Because I was in my sleeping bag.
3. Because Ellie was looking at me like I was nuts.
4. Because there was no mutant croc.

"What? Hey? Who? Mnaagnaaarghnn," I said. And no, I don't know what that "Mnaagnaaarghnn" thing was, either. It just sort of came out like that: kind of somewhere between a shriek and a moan. A shroan.

GREAAAAAT, way to go impressing Ellie, Rafe! *Siiiiigh.*

"You were having a nightmare," Ellie said.

How. Embarrassing.

But wait! It gets worse…

"It was a pretty big one," she added, "judging by all that screaming. You scream like a little kid, by the way."

UGH!

"A three-year-old, in fact," she said. "I can't believe I'm the only one who woke up."

Ugh, ugh, uuuuuugh!

"Thanks for pointing that out," I said. I'm surprised I got out any words. I guess I was too tired to be embarrassed into silence. Or freaked out.

That dream was scary!

I carefully surveyed the camp. The dream had been so *real* that I still half-expected the croc to reappear any second. I reached down and patted myself to check but my legs were still there. I sank back into my swag and closed my eyes.

"Wait," Ellie said, punching me on the arm. "You have to come with me."

I opened one eye experimentally. "I do? Where?"

What I almost said was, "Okay! Anywhere you want!"

But I half expected Ellie to be making fun of me again.

"I need to go to the bathroom and I don't want to go out there alone." She stood up. "C'mon, be a gentleman."

Um, okay?

I'd like to say I got to my feet gracefully and took her arm and led her into the wilderness to take a leak. But what actually happened was that I scrambled to my feet, nearly tripped over my sleeping bag, and by the time I'd gotten myself together, Ellie had marched off without me.

Sighing, I followed her. I couldn't blame Ellie for wanting company. It was cold now—real cold—and all that big dark nothing surrounding us looked about as inviting as a haunted castle during a thunderstorm.

Plus, I could probably go, too. There had been a moment in my croc nightmare when...Anyway, there's no need for me to go into detail. Let's just say it had been a close call.

CHAPTER 31

PEEING IS OVERRATED

Using my phone as a flashlight, we walked about two hundred feet from camp until we reached some scrubby plants. I would have been happy to pee somewhere *a lot* closer to camp, but Ellie just *had* to do it behind a bush.

"Can I borrow your phone?" Ellie asked.

"Um," I said, immediately spotting the major problem with Ellie's plan. "That means I'll be here in the dark. Alone. And I need to pee, too."

"So pee," Ellie said. "Don't be such a wuss." She grabbed my phone before I could argue and scurried behind the bushes.

I bit back what I was going to say. *Be tough, Rafe,* I told myself. But what can I say, I wasn't tough, I was scared.

The clouds had rolled in, blocking the starlight and making things pretty dark. I didn't want to pee right next to Ellie—that'd be weird—so I walked to a rise in the ground near a small creek. With a last look to check Ellie was nowhere in sight, I stood on the rise and started peeing. As I was reaching the finish line (you know what I mean), I felt the ground move beneath my feet.

"Whoa!" I said, struggling to keep my balance *and* not pee on my feet. (Dudes, if you've ever had to pee on a moving train, you'll know how this feels.)

I frowned. Were we having an earthquake?

Oh crud, we were having an earthquake!!!

Then it stopped. So okay, maybe it was over…?

I finished up and turned to see a light coming toward me, the beam from the phone swinging back and forth across the desert floor.

"Ellie?" I said.

"Where are you?" she called.

"Over here on the hill."

Ellie swung the beam of light in my direction just as the ground moved again.

"You feel that?" I asked.

Her eyes widened. "Uh, Rafe..."

"Like an earth tremor or something," I said.

"Rafe," Ellie said slowly, "don't panic, but..."

Is it just me, or when people say "don't panic," do you immediately start panicking, too?

"But what?!"

"It's not the ground that's moving." Ellie pointed the beam of light at my feet.

Uh-oh.

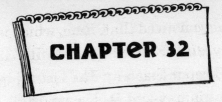

CHAPTER 32

WHATEVER YOU DO, DON'T WAKE THE CROCODILE

Have you ever been told you're standing on a giant crocodile? Didn't think so. Not many people have.

Well, I can now tell you, from practical, firsthand knowledge, that it is not a life experience I'd wish on my worst enemy (Principal Stricker) or one that I'd like to repeat anytime in, say, the next eight thousand years.

And I swear, this time it *really was happening*.

I even pinched myself to see if I'd wake up. But I didn't.

"Don't. Move. A. Muscle," Ellie said quietly.

"*What do you mean 'don't move'?*" I hissed. "In case you hadn't noticed, I'm standing on a giant crocodile!"

"Yes, I *have* noticed that, Rafe, which is why you have to stay *still*!" Ellie whispered. "It's *asleep*, so we need to keep it that way. The last thing we need is an awake giant crocodile! I've heard these things can move pretty fast. If you jump off, you might stumble, trip on a rock or something."

I wanted to point out that I WOULDN'T do that. But let's be honest, everyone who knows me also knows that I definitely would.

"And then," Ellie continued, "you'll be croc breakfast before you can say 'bacon and eggs.' It doesn't even have to eat you. It might just bite off a leg."

I gulped. Ellie had a point—a *good* point.

I didn't want to be anyone's breakfast. And I liked my legs just the way they were. Attached to me.

So great, good, all this was useful information but it didn't change the fact that I WAS STILL STANDING ON A CROCODILE.

The entire time this was going on, I'd been avoiding looking at the crocodile on the (really dumb) basis that what you don't see can't hurt you. I risked a quick glance down and nearly lost it for real.

The thing was *enormous*.

Okay, it wasn't as big as the mutant flying croc in my nightmare but it was still an absolutely freaking *massive* thing full of sharp teeth and strong jaws.

Are there even crocodiles in California?

Random Fact #458:

Crocodiles are 168 times more dangerous than sharks.

Sharks! 168! How was that even possible?

"What am I going to do?" I whispered, trying and failing to keep the panic out of my voice.

168!

CHAPTER 33

THAT'S THE PLAN?

I wanted to burst out crying but two things stopped me. First, Ellie was there and, as we've established, me looking like an idiot and/or baby = embarrassing. (That's right, folks, RK is more afraid of being embarrassed than of being eaten.) And, second, it might wake the croc.

Ellie paused.

That wasn't a good sign. I had kind of figured that Ellie, being Ellie, would have some snappy plan at her fingertips. But all I got was a pause. A pause was the last thing I needed.

"Uh, Ellie?"

"I'm *thinking*," she said, frowning. "Give me a minute."

A minute of waiting patiently while standing on

the back of a sleeping crocodile isn't easy. Let's just say, if all the things in the universe were ranked from hardest to easiest, standing on a ferocious croc would be somewhere at the top. Waaaay at the top.

The seconds ticked past like years.

"Anytime," I whispered fiercely. "I'll just be right here."

"Okay," Ellie said, a determined expression on her face. There was a gleam in her eye that I liked. She was doing a good impression of someone who had just thought of a brilliant idea. This was more like it. I waited to hear her plan, sure that it would be fantastic.

"Run," she said finally. "Really fast."

"Okay, great! I'll...Wait, WHAT?" I said. "Run? That's *it*? That's your big plan?"

"Don't forget the really fast part," Ellie said. "That's the most important thing."

"That's the worst plan I've ever heard!" I wanted to scream, but since I still had no desire to become crocodile food, I had to make do with whispering really, really loud and looking incredibly angry.

"What did you expect me to do?" Ellie asked. "Build a helicopter from whatever I can find in this *completely empty desert*? Assemble a tranquilizer crossbow from your earwax and my hair? Make a—"

"Okay, okay! I get it."

I steadied myself. Ellie was right. Kind of. It was the best we were going to come up with. "So I just hop off and run?"

Ellie nodded. "Uh-huh. *Fast.*"

I noticed she'd backed up a few steps, which didn't exactly fill me with confidence. I should point out that, although there had been a weird moment back at Hills Village when I played football for the school (yes, really), I'm not what you'd call "athletic." I mean, I can run pretty fast when required—and now was one of those times—but I also knew I was more than capable of falling flat on my face. Especially in the dark.

168!

"On the count of three," Ellie said, taking another step back. "One..."

Right then, the crocodile woke up. It made the sort of sound you'd expect a hungry crocodile to make and twisted its head around to see what kind of midnight snack was standing on its back.

"Twothree!" I screamed, and leaped out into space.

CHAPTER 34

DON'T LOOK BACK

Right, let's get it out of the way now:
I didn't fall on my face.

In fact, I didn't fall. PERIOD!

I know you all thought I would, but I didn't.
Ha! Are you disappointed? Thought it might
be fun seeing me get caught by the croc like
Captain Hook? Well, sorry to disappoint, but
I managed to stay on my feet and run like I'd
never run before.

I mean, c'mon, if *you* were jumping off the back
of a giant crocodile in the dead of night in the
middle of the California desert, would *you* fall?

Didn't think so.

I hit the dirt with the precision of a circus
trapeze artist and took off like a gazelle with its

tail on fire before the croc had a chance to figure out what was happening.

You're so agile, Rafe!

"RUN!" I yelled as I sprinted toward Ellie.

I looked over my shoulder. The croc might have started slow but it had got its bearings now and was coming after us fast.

"It's catching up!" Ellie yelled. "There's no way we can run faster than that croc!"

"I know," I said, putting on a spurt and breezing past her like an Olympic sprinter straining for the tape, "but all I have to do is make sure I run faster than *you*!"

I just wanted to put a joke in there to lighten the mood a little because I have to tell you: being chased by a giant croc is super crummy.

I mean, there was stomach-churning excitement like the kind you get when you watch a scary movie, except this *wasn't* a scary movie. This was all-too-real life...and so mainly I was upset at the idea of getting eaten.

By now Ellie and I were running as fast as we could side by side, which was about half the speed we needed to go. We had no idea which direction we were moving in and every step we took in the dark increased the chances of tripping over a rock and becoming croc food.

Behind us, the croc scrabbled across the dirt, the noise getting louder and louder with every step.

Boofboom, boofboom, boofboom.

Even though I was panicking like crazy, a tiny part of me felt a little tickle of curiosity. That *boofboom* sound was very close to the sound I'd heard in my nightmare. But how could that be?

How could I possibly know what a giant crocodile sounded like?

Unless—and this was a really scary idea—I had heard the croc moving around the campsite while I was sleeping and had somehow mixed that into my nightmare!

I shook the idea out of my head. None of that was helping us right now.

"I don't think I can keep this up much longer," I panted.

Ellie didn't reply. I didn't blame her. That joke about only needing to outrun each other wasn't so funny now. Both of us knew we didn't have much time left unless something very dramatic happened.

Or else we were crocodile food.

CHAPTER 35

PANT, PANT, PANT

At the exact moment when I thought I couldn't run another step, the croc stopped dead in its tracks, like a switch had been pressed. One second he'd been *boofboom*ing after us like crazy, the next he was slinking back to the creek, fading into the darkness with each heavy step.

We jogged to a halt.

"That. Was. Close," I panted.

My legs felt like they were made of marshmallow. If that croc changed its mind and came back for another run at us, I wouldn't stand a chance.

"No. Kidding," Ellie said, gasping for air. "I. Thought. We. Were. Goners."

A couple of minutes later we had recovered enough to think about getting back to Camp Culture. Ellie suggested we head away from the creek and go around in a big circle. She seemed to have a better idea about where the camp was, and it wasn't like I was going to disagree with any suggestion that took us *away* from the croc.

"Let's make it a really big circle," I said. "Like, a *really,* really big one."

As far as I was concerned, we could go via Mars if it meant not risking a close encounter of the croc kind.

We walked in silence for a while, both of us (probably) thinking about our near death experience. Me (definitely) thinking about how I could've impressed her by saving her from the croc...and how I hadn't.

"You'd think McGarrity would have warned us about the croc," I said eventually. "I mean, he might be a bit of a blowhard but he wouldn't want us to actually get eaten, would he? And if he's spent so much time around here because of those cave paintings, wouldn't he know there were crocs around?"

"Actually," Ellie said, "I've never heard of a crocodile being in California."

"Isn't California known for having a lot of crocodile attacks?" I asked.

"That's Florida, and it's mainly alligators," Ellie said.

"Oh, right."

And I was back to looking like an idiot in front of Ellie.

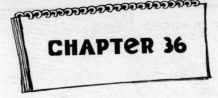

CHAPTER 36

ON THE PLUS SIDE,
NO ONE GOT EATEN

When we got back to Camp Culture, we decided that one of us would stay awake for a couple of hours and keep watch, then swap over.

"I'll go first," I said, kind of hoping Ellie would put up an argument. Or at least notice I was being generous.

She didn't do either.

"Okay," she said, and went straight to sleep.

So much for that.

I rubbed my face and did my best security guard impression.

I did a loop around the campfire, found a rock to lean against, and...

...woke up feeling like someone had taken out my brain. For a few seconds I didn't know *who* I was, let alone where and why.

"Nice job, Sleeping Beauty," Ellie said, as she came into view. I squinted up at her. She put her hands on her hips and looked down at me like I was something unpleasant she couldn't scrape off her shoe, and behind her was the bright, morning sun.

"Weren't you supposed to keep watch and then wake me up?" Ellie asked.

What could I say?

I'd meant to stay awake, honest.

"On the plus side," I said, "no one got eaten...?"

Ellie just rolled her eyes.

I got up, and together we went to find out what there was for breakfast. Fortunately, I hadn't missed it!

After we got food, it was decided we'd all go swimming before the art stuff. That was fine with me. I don't think I would've been able to concentrate on drawing after the night I had.

But...

The place Brushes took us to was a kind of

swimming hole in a creek, where the water is nice and shallow. It was a cool pool of blue water curling around a bend in the creek with a few green trees (the only green thing for miles around) arcing toward the surface. And it looked great...apart from one tiny detail.

Crocodiles could be in there.

"Go swimming?" I gulped. Now I had a whole new croc-shaped worry.

"That's the idea, Ralph," Brushes said.

I ignored him and glanced at Ellie. "Uh, I don't

think that's a good idea," I said. "What about crocodiles?"

Brushes laughed.

Mrs. Donatello frowned and said, "There aren't any crocodiles around here, Rafe."

"Actually," I said, "that's not strictly true."

Brushes glowered at me. "What?"

"We saw one," I said. "Last night. I, uh, needed to pee and so did Ellie. While we were out there, well, like I said, that's when we saw one. A croc, that is."

For some reason I didn't mention I'd been *standing* on the back of the croc having a leak when I'd noticed. I don't know, out in the cold light of day—or even the baking hot sun of midafternoon—not noticing when you're standing on the back of a three-ton croc seems a little dumb.

"Rafe," Mrs. Donatello said, sounding disappointed.

I started to tell her I wasn't making it up, but Brushes said, "You sure about this?" His voice got even growlier than usual. It sounded like he'd been chewing sandpaper. "It's real dark out there, kiddo. Your mind plays tricks. A non-Californian like you might have confused a boulder out there for an actual crocodile. This place isn't nicknamed Crocodile Rocks for nothin'."

"I never saw any rocks that look like crocodiles when we went to the paintings," Ellie pointed out.

"You just haven't been looking close enough," Brushes said.

I shook my head. "Uh, nope, we definitely saw a—"

"You know, Brushes might be right, Rafe," Ellie said, suddenly backing off her McGarrity interrogation. "We could have mistaken Crocodile Rocks for a real one."

"*What?*" I stared at her in disbelief. I'd been *standing* on one—of course it was real!

But Ellie gave me a wink and I realized something was up...

CHAPTER 37

EPIC FAIL

That night, Ellie and I got to work.

See, we'd made a plan while everyone else was swimming. I didn't go in the water. Even though I was 100 percent sure the croc from last night wasn't going to show up—okay, maybe like 98 percent sure—I still didn't like the idea of dipping so much as one toe in a California puddle.

But anyway, back to Ellie's and my idea.

The light bulb thing? Really?

Our big idea might not've been the greatest, come to think of it. But when the girl you're crushing on wants to go exploring in the dark looking for a crocodile, you do it.

Yeah, THAT was our grand plan. Find the croc and get a picture of it this time. Then everyone would *have* to believe us.

Either that or we'd be crocodile food.

We didn't find much. It was all mega anticlimactic. But then I got to thinking. Maybe this whole nighttime trip through the wilderness didn't have to be for nothing. I was with Ellie, after all.

And that's when I got another GREAT IDEA.

(Okay, even I'll admit that this one wasn't so great.)

I decided to tell Ellie how I felt.

"Hey, so…"

Ellie shone her flashlight in my face. I squinted and held up an arm. "What?" she asked. "You see something?"

"No. Nothing." Literally. I couldn't see anything now, thanks to her blinding me. I blinked until I could *kinda* see. "I wanted to talk to you about something."

"Oookay. But I think we should be quiet if we want to find the crocs, you know?"

"Yeah, but…I like you, and…*Like you* like you, so…"

I grew old, withered away, and died waiting for her to respond. And when she finally, *finally*, FINALLY said something, it was this:

"Shhh!"

WHAT.

Had she not heard me?

Did I not actually say that out loud? It *was* possible.

She dragged me to the ground. "Look."

She pointed to her left, at lights on the horizon. They were very faint but definitely there. It could only be one thing.

"Aliens!" I yelped.

Like my epic fail couldn't get any more epic.

CHAPTER 38

ALIENS SHMALIENS

A liens?" Ellie said, arching an eyebrow at me. I could tell from her tone that she didn't think I was right.

"Uh, maybe," I said. "It's possible."

"Unlikely," Ellie said. "But that would be cool, huh?"

Cool? Not exactly what I'd been thinking, but I nodded because if Ellie thought what I'd said was cool, then maybe she thought *I* was cool. Kind of.

"Let's take a closer look," she said.

As we got to the top of a rise in the ground, we saw that the lights were heading toward a rock formation. The lights were too far away to see properly but I could tell it was probably a car or a truck—not aliens.

"I thought there was nothing much out here," I said.

Ellie pointed to our right. "That's not all."

From our new viewpoint we could see more lights coming from what looked like a crack in the ground. These lights were nearer but had been hidden from view until we'd shifted position.

Maybe these were the aliens. I was still pretty sure aliens might be out here.

We moved quietly to the edge of a ravine that formed a long V-shaped clearing. In the middle of the clearing was a large, shiny trailer, the kind of thing Tom Cruise would have on a movie set. Not that I'd ever been on a movie set, but I COULD'VE BEEN if we'd gone to Hollywood instead of the wilderness! But I was sure this trailer would fit right in.

Two cars with tinted windows and white logos on the doors were parked at angles to the trailer, and behind it was a large rectangular box under a tarpaulin. Ellie pulled out her phone and snapped a couple of photos, taking care to turn off the flash. Outside the trailer, talking in low voices and sitting on lounge chairs around a campfire, were four men. Two were dressed in black fleece jackets, but I still easily recognized them as a couple of the suits from the reception at the Bigbottom Creek Hotel three nights ago. Both of them wore sunglasses even though it was dark out. Weird.

The other two men were Brushes and Vern.

Brushes leaned back in his lounge chair and swirled the ice in his glass before taking a long, satisfying swig. He stretched his feet a little closer to the fire and wiggled his toes.

"So much for roughing it," Ellie murmured. "The big phony."

"I don't get it," I whispered back. "Why all the secrecy?"

"And why are those blokes out here?" Ellie said. "They don't exactly look like the outdoors type."

We both went quiet when Brushes started talking.

"We'll just have to keep looking," he said. "It's there—it has to be."

"MegaGlobal won't stay away forever," one of the sunglasses guys said. "They'll find a way around your little painting stunt."

"Exactly, so we need to get in and get out— *now*," Brushes said.

Ellie and I looked at each other. What were they talking about?

I leaned forward, trying to get a better view of that weird, giant box poking out from behind the trailer—but I knocked into Ellie, who let out a tiny yelp. Both of us froze.

"What was that?" Vern asked.

"Go check it out," Brushes said.

Ellie and I took that as our cue to get out of there—fast!

CHAPTER 39

THE KID WHO COULD

Yᴏu know that feeling when you're trying to think of something and it's right on the tip of your tongue, only you can't quite squeeze it out? *That* was what this was. We almost had enough info to figure out what was going on, but not enough to *actually* figure it out. It's the most annoying thing in the world!

What were Brushes and those guys talking about?

What was in that huge box?

What was going on here?

If I got it right, the whole thing went something like this:

1. If Brushes *was* up to something shady in the caves, even he wouldn't risk the lives of all us kids if there was a *chance* of a crocodile around...

2. ...which meant that Brushes knew—not guessed—that the crocodile was nowhere to be seen because...

3. ...the croc was safely locked up in the box behind the trailer.

I didn't have proof, but I knew that something fishier than a truckload of sardines was going on. Between the croc that wasn't supposed to be in California, the cave paintings that were supposed to be super old but smelled like fresh paint, and then the weird suit dudes Brushes and Vern were hanging out with. And then whatever they were talking about. Getting something before something called MegaGlobal got it first? What was *that* all about?

It had to do with the cave paintings, probably. "Get in and get out" sounded like going into the caves. But why would the paintings be fake? And did Brushes know they were fake? Had he put them there or had he gotten fooled by them?

I felt like there was a big, really complicated jigsaw puzzle laid out in front of me with the important pieces there…but all in the wrong places. I needed information from the outside world if Rafe Khatchadorian, Ace Detective, was going to crack the Case of the California Croc and the Forged Cave Paintings wide open. And since we were stuck out here for another few days, it didn't look likely that I'd be able to find out anything.

But I knew a kid who could.

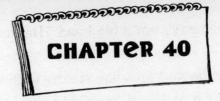

CHAPTER 40

SUPER-SECRET SPY NETWORK

The next day, every time Ellie and I looked up from talking, we'd find Brushes glancing at us from underneath his face fungus. Time dragged, mainly because Brushes decided to "encourage creativity" by getting Vloot to make a clay bust... using Brushes as a model.

"Man, that guy's got a big head," Denny whispered.

He and Ellie and me were sitting with our backs against a rock with our feet pointed toward the firepit.

"I don't know," I said, peering at Vloot's sculpture. "I think it looks about right."

"No," Denny said, "I mean only a big head would get someone to make a statue of himself, right?"

It wasn't exactly a statue but Denny was right. There was something kind of odd about the whole thing.

"I don't think Vloot wanted to do it, either," Ellie said. "I heard Brushes sort of *insisting*. Weird."

Finally, Brushes got tired of sitting still and went off somewhere. Said he was going to get some firewood for later, but I was pretty sure that was just an excuse and he was really going to the fifty-foot LuxCamp G6 "Executive Range" air-conditioned trailer hidden in a secret ravine.

Now that Brushes was out of earshot, it was time at last for my super-secret spy network to spring into action.

Okay, my super-secret spy network was just

Denny. But Denny had said he was a hacker, so now was his time to prove it.

In about ten minutes flat he'd got all the information we needed.

Turns out he really knew what he was doing.

"MegaGlobal Industries," he read, "is the second-largest mining operation in the world. And here's where it gets really interesting: MegaGlobal owns these mountains. There were a bunch of rumors about some Native American cave paintings, but no one had ever seen any until a few weeks ago when McGarrity discovered them in a place he called 'Crocodile Rocks.'"

"So wait," I said, "*he* named the caves that?"

"Looks like it," Denny said, peering at the screen.

"I still don't get what we heard them talking about," Ellie said. "What are McGarrity and those suits trying to find before MegaGlobal does?"

"More cave paintings?" I suggested.

"Okay, but *why*?" Ellie asked. "What good does that do them?"

None of us could answer that.

"They said 'it' anyway," Ellie added. "And talked about the paintings being faked."

"Oh, hey," Denny said, still looking at his screen, "you know that diamond that went missing?"

"The Bluebird-something?" Ellie asked.

"Brilliant Bluebird, yeah," he said. "It's rumored to have disappeared around here!"

"Okay, but what about the crocodile?" I said. Who cared about a diamond when we could get EATEN?

That's what I thought back then, anyway. But maybe I should've been paying more attention.

"Who brought the croc in?" I asked.
"MegaGlobal or McGarrity?" I'd been pretty sure
it was Brushes, but maybe we were blaming
everything on him when it wasn't all his fault...

Another image flashed up on the screen, this
time showing the logo of a trucking company. "Big
Critters Trucking," Denny said. "Specializes in
the transportation of large animals. Crocodiles a
specialty."

Ellie and I peered at the computer as Denny
brought up another webpage, which had a picture
of a large rectangular cage that looked exactly
the size of the box behind McGarrity's trailer.

"The ReptoHouse XXL Cage costs eight hundred dollars and one was ordered by a McGarrity, B, of Bigbottom Creek last month. Look familiar? I'm figuring that McGarrity is using the tame croc to keep people's noses out of Crocodile Rocks."

Ellie looked up at us. "Something tells me we might need to go and take a look at the ravine again."

CHAPTER 41

MEAT

A rmed with Denny's information, which slotted plenty of missing pieces into the jigsaw, the three of us headed out into the desert again once it was dark and everybody else was asleep.

Denny had discovered that five hundred pounds of meat had been shipped out a few days before the camp started. We figured that this could be for the croc, which meant, in theory, that it shouldn't be that hungry.

In theory.

I'm absolutely stuffed.

To be honest, I would have felt a whole bunch better if we really *had* been special agent types, but, out there in the dark, we were just three artsy nerds with some wild ideas, all of which could be as far off the mark as the size of the Pacific Ocean. Maybe finding out what Brushes McGarrity and MegaGlobal Industries were up to—or if they were up to anything at all—was way out of our reach.

Despite all this kind of sort of possibly being my idea, I now wasn't sure I wanted to get *this* serious about it all.

On the one hand, it did look very much like something was going on out at Crocodile Rocks and that McGarrity was in it up to his bristly red neck. But on the other hand, it really wasn't any of my business.

This certainly crossed the line of my mom's one request: "Don't get into trouble, Rafe!" In fact, this was so far over the line I couldn't even see it anymore.

Line, what line?

Once we were close to the ravine, Ellie said, "There. See the light?"

Denny, who had missed all the "fun" when we were out here last night, took a moment to see what Ellie was pointing out. "Okay, got it," he said.

We slowly moved forward. I could feel my breath quickening and told myself to relax.

I'd been in these situations before. I was, after all, a Man of Experience.

At the edge of the ravine, we lay down on our bellies and wriggled to the lip of the cliff. Just like last night, Brushes was sitting on a sun lounger, chatting with the men in suits. I swallowed hard as I looked at the empty crocodile cage. Full croc belly or not, being out here with a thing like that was no joke.

Ellie nudged my elbow and gestured for us to drop back. With Brushes and the Suits safely tucked up at the ravine, it was time for us to take a closer look at what was going on over at Crocodile Rocks.

CHAPTER 42

ROCK AND ROLL

It took us about an hour to get to Crocodile Rocks and that hour was right up there with the lousiest ones of my life.

We were on foot, and in the dark, and the whole time we were out there, there was the very real possibility of bumping into that croc…So, all things considered, it wasn't exactly a stroll in the park.

Plus, Denny and Ellie didn't seem to be so worried and they talked the whole way. A lot. She even laughed at something stupid he said. I kicked at the ground and followed behind them.

I'd have been happier dancing into Principal Stricker's office wearing a chicken costume.

Eventually, we arrived at a spot where we could see what was going on. We climbed carefully up a rocky slope, toward a ledge that overlooked the area where we'd seen the lights disappear the previous night.

"Whoa," Denny said as we all looked down. "Check it out."

The lights at Crocodile Rocks weren't coming from cars—they were coming from trucks. *Lots* of trucks. In fact, judging by the amount of vehicles going in and out, there was a totally serious operation going on down there.

"Looks like McGarrity means business," Ellie

said. She lifted her camera to her eye and started filming.

"Seems pretty busy for a place that's supposed to be closed," I agreed.

Denny unpacked his mobile satellite kit. "We have to get this on the internet," he said.

"Wait," a rock next to Denny said. "Not so fast."

We all froze.

Whatthefreakin'whatwhat?

Now, I don't know about you, but when a rock starts talking, it kind of gives you a shock. And yup, that's what had happened. A *rock* had just spoke.

As far as I was concerned there were only three possibilities:

1. This wasn't actually happening. Maybe I was having one of my fantasy moments, or

2. We had stumbled into a parallel universe, or

3. There really *was* a rock talking to us.

I was kind of edging toward the parallel universe theory when the rock began to move, and I stopped trying to make sense of what was happening. We watched, paralyzed with fear, as the rock got to its feet (yup, the thing had feet) and stood, silhouetted against the truck lights coming from Crocodile Rocks. Small stones and dust cascaded down from the creature's head and skitter-scattered across the ground. It was something straight out of a horror movie.

And I wasn't making it up. I swear!

"RUN!" Denny yelled.

Ellie and I scrabbled frantically to escape. As I stumbled down the slope, I turned back to see the rock monster's hand coming down on Denny's shoulder. I skidded to a halt. We couldn't just leave him.

I could rescue him and look like a hero in front of Ellie…

"Get out of here!" Denny cried out as he struggled helplessly in the rock monster's granite grip. It was the bravest thing I'd ever seen.

Certainly braver than the bravest thing I'd ever done (which, for the record, was the time I'd insulted Miller the Killer right to his face).

"We can't just go!" I said.

"Stop!" the rock monster growled. With Denny firmly in its grip, the creature took a step toward us.

"Aaaargh!" Ellie screamed and ran.

Okay, confession time: it was actually me who screamed and ran, and Ellie was the one who didn't want to leave. But she wasn't far behind when I started running. Being brave was one thing, but being caught by a rock monster was another.

I didn't even know what a rock monster would *do* in that situation.

Eat me? Crush me? Crush me and then eat me?

Turn me into rock? One thing was for sure:

I didn't want to hang around to find out. I felt sorry for Denny—like, *really, really* sorry—but there was no way Ellie and I could fight a thing like that. *It was made of rock!* Our only chance was to get back to the ravine and raise the alarm. Whatever scheme Brushes and the Suits were up to would have to wait until we'd tried to save Denny.

Denny didn't reply. Instead, I heard a horrible grinding sound that I never, ever wanted to hear again.

I kept running and didn't look back.

CHAPTER 43

THIS IS BARRY

It's hard enough trying to find your way around a desert at night without having to worry about crocodiles. Add a mutant killer rock monster to the mix and there's only going to be one result: we got lost. It might have taken us an hour to get to Crocodile Rocks, but it took us *waaaay* longer to get back.

The adrenaline had left us both feeling weak as kittens. We were covered in dust and our ankles were bruised and scratched from our panicky getaway. Eventually, though, we saw the lights from the ravine and picked up the pace. We were sure that Denny had been crunched or eaten or turned into rock himself by now but we still had to let some grown-ups know. I just hoped that when Mrs. Donatello relayed all this to my mom and Principal Stricker I wouldn't be in *too* much trouble.

Who am I kidding? I was gonna be in HUGE trouble.

About a hundred feet from the ravine, Denny stepped out from behind a rock.

"Hi," he said.

This is how surprised we looked:

I think I would have passed out if I hadn't been so relieved.

"Denny!" I yelled, grabbing his shoulders to check he was real. "You're alive!"

Denny put a finger to his lips. "Quiet. And yes, I'm alive."

"What happened?" Ellie said. "The last we saw that…that *thing* had hold of you!"

"Riiiiight," Denny said. "It's probably easier to show you than explain. Just don't freak out, okay?" He moved back to the rock he'd been hiding behind. "This is Barry."

"*What* is Barry?" I asked, thinking Denny's experience must have scrambled his brain.

"Me," said the rock, moving forward and putting out a hand. "Delighted to meet you."

CHAPTER 44

FREAK-OUT TIME

The rock monster held out his hand.

What else could I do? Leaving the rock monster hanging would have been really rude. "Rafe," I replied, shaking it.

I didn't freak out, but I got real close to it for a couple of seconds.

The rock monster had human hands, and now that I had a chance to look more closely I could see that the rock monster was actually a dude wearing some pretty convincing desert camouflage.

"Barry's been doing the same as us," Denny explained. "He's trying to find out what's happening at Crocodile Rocks. He's a photographer."

Barry held up an expensive-looking camera

with a long zoom lens. "I was pretty close tonight," he said. He took off his headgear and I could see Barry was a guy about thirty years old. Or maybe fifty.

To be honest, I can't really tell how old grown-ups are—especially when they're disguised as a rock.

"Things have been getting busier around here over the past few weeks, so MegaGlobal has been getting sloppy. I think I might have got something on the camera tonight but I'm not sure," Barry said.

Denny tapped his bag of digital goodies. "Only one way to find out."

At a quiet spot, not too far from Camp Culture, Denny downloaded Barry's pictures.

Most of them were shots of the inside of the entrance to Crocodile Rocks but they were all either too grainy or too fuzzy or too dark to see much of anything.

"Useless," Barry said. He kicked a nearby stone, sending it flying across the desert. "I really thought tonight…" He trailed off miserably. He looked about as sad as someone dressed as a rock could look, which, for the record, is pretty sad.

Denny leaned back and flexed his fingers. "Don't panic just yet, man," he said. "Stand back and watch a master at work."

We watched as his fingers flew over the keyboard, feeding the images through different filters. After a minute or two, he stopped suddenly.

"What is it?" Ellie asked.

On-screen was a close-up of the inside of the cave. Most of the photo showed the back of a workman's head and the side mirror of a truck heading out of the cave.

"Those aren't MegaGlobal guys," Ellie said. "Look—their hats have a different logo on them!"

Sure enough, she was right. But if these people weren't working for MegaGlobal, then who were they working for?

"And what's that?" I asked, pointing at a stack of something next to the truck.

Denny tapped a key three times and the image sharpened. And there, sitting in a pile, were paint cans with paint dripping down the sides.

Brushes McGarrity, Cousin Vern, and the Suits *were* up to something!

We wanted to yell and shout but, because we had to keep everything quiet, we had to dance around silently, grinning like chimpanzees and waving our arms.

If that croc had wandered past right then, he'd have had second thoughts about attacking such a bunch of Froot Loops.

Once we'd calmed down a bit, we put the story together.

"So McGarrity forged the paintings," Barry said, "to prevent MegaGlobal from doing anything with Crocodile Rocks, since if there are Native American paintings, they'll need to be preserved and the company won't be able to mine here."

"Why would such a big mining company bother with an area like Crocodile Rocks?" Ellie asked. "It's too small to develop into something worthwhile."

"And why is Brushes here faking paintings to stop MegaGlobal from going into caves?" I asked. *With a man-eating crocodile!*

"Because," Barry said, "they're looking for diamonds."

"In California?" Ellie asked, crossing her arms. "There are no diamonds here."

"Exactly," Barry said. "But there's one particular diamond that just might be."

CHAPTER 45

THE LEGEND OF THE BRILLIANT BLUEBIRD DIAMOND

One hundred years ago, a bright-blue diamond was uncovered during an archeological dig.

The diamond was placed in a museum and known as the Mighty Azure Eagle Flame of the Mountains.

But it was better known as the **Brilliant Bluebird.**

Then the diamond was stolen- and promptly lost by the thieves. Rumor has it, the diamond is around here somewhere, since this is where the thieves ran off to. But it still hasn't been found.

CHAPTER 46

DOES BARRY THE ROCK MONSTER EXIST?

Before leaving Barry, we decided someone should call the police. I wasn't volunteering, and neither was Ellie or Denny, but Barry said he'd do it. Then we left. There wasn't much else to do. So we went back to camp and tried to sleep.

It was easier than you might think.

My head hit my pillow and I was out.

After a sleep so deep you'd have needed a nuclear-powered sub to wake me, I unglued my eyelids and lay back on my sleeping bag, looking up at a cloudy sky.

Clouds.

That was good.

I had never properly appreciated clouds until I went to the desert. With clouds around, today might not feel like I was an overdone brownie on the top shelf of the oven at Swifty's.

My throat felt like a porcupine had bedded down in there for the night and, without checking, I just knew this was a bad hair day to end all bad hair days.

I had dreamed plenty but none of my dreams were as straight up *crazycakes* as what had happened last night.

Or *had* it happened?

Was it possible I'd imagined everything?

Did Barry the rock monster exist? Had we really uncovered evidence that Brushes McGarrity had faked cave paintings so he could find the Brilliant Bluebird Diamond out from under MegaGlobal Industries' nose? Had I missed breakfast?

It turned out I hadn't, which was good because I was so hungry I could almost have eaten a sardine sandwich.

Almost.

I staggered across to the food tent and took a seat at the table, trying to figure out last night.

Eric and Monique were just finishing up and they told me that today we'd all be doing our art. There would be no trips and no organized events. Brushes had taken off somewhere, which suited me just fine since I wasn't looking forward to keeping my mouth shut all day.

Vern clattered a stack of bacon, eggs, and pancakes the size of NYC down in front of me. There was so much food on my plate that if it fell over it could easily injure someone, so I spent a happy forty-two seconds relocating the pancakes to a safer location—my stomach.

I'll say this for Big Vern: he might be a great hulking, dumb henchman but he sure knew how to drive a griddle.

Eric and Monique left, and while I ate I watched Vloot working on the sculpture of Brushes McGarrity. Somewhere from out behind the camp, I could hear what sounded like two cats fighting in a washing machine. I figured Yrsa was doing some experimenting. Linda had spread out a sheet of plastic and was grinding rocks into some kind of paint. There was no sign of Thiago and, judging from the snores coming from their swags, Ellie and Denny were still fast asleep.

This was how I'd kind of imagined the camp to be when I'd first got the invitation: everyone doing their artsy thing.

While we were waiting for news from Barry,

that's what I'd do, too: art. After all, I wasn't here
to do battle with mining companies.

  I was an artist.

CHAPTER 47

ONE OF OUR KIDS IS MISSING

I found a quiet spot and started working on some paintings. It was a night scene of Crocodile Rocks. I hadn't done much art in a while, so it felt good to lose myself in it.

From time to time I glanced up and saw Ellie and Denny chatting. Of course they were. They'd become great friends all of a sudden. I felt weird about that, a weird I didn't like.

I kept watching them, but I didn't go over to them. There was nothing stopping me, but I just sat there, getting annoyed as I worked on my art. After a while, I saw them walk over to where Thiago's stuff was. Something about the way they were standing made me put down my paintbrush. This was different. Denny bent down and looked at the ground. He said something to Ellie.

I walked over to them, a bad feeling growing in the pit of my stomach right next to that stack of pancakes—a different bad feeling than what I felt watching Ellie and Denny earlier. Now that I thought about it, I hadn't seen Thiago since yesterday.

"What is it?" I said when I reached Thiago's stuff.

Ellie pointed at the ground. I couldn't see much, just some footprints and marks in the red dirt.

"What?" I said.

Denny pulled me over to a couple of tracks about a shoulder width apart. He squatted down and pointed at the dirt. "Looks to me like someone's dragged Thiago off somewhere," he said. "Look, here are some finger marks—that'd be Thiago. Large feet here and here, and two drag tracks going up and over there."

"How did you work that out?" I said, impressed even though I was annoyed with Denny right now.

"Crooked Case Histories," Denny replied. "I love that show. They had one on a beach where a dude had been dragged off his lounger chair."

"The big question is," Ellie said, "what's happened to Thiago?"

Denny shrugged. "Only one way to find out."

I wanted to point out that we could *probably* come up with a second or third way if we thought hard enough, but Ellie and Denny were already following the trail, so I ran after them. We left Camp Culture and headed toward the creek. I didn't want to look like a chicken in front of Ellie. But I really hoped we wouldn't run into something big and hungry.

"I don't like this one little bit," Ellie said. She was filming the tracks and I had a quick flash forward—*frrrrp!*—to a courtroom with her footage being shown as evidence.

Denny, who was a little in front of us, suddenly stopped. He bent down and came back up with a ripped piece of cloth.

"What's that?" Ellie asked.

The tattered yellow-and-green cloth hung from Denny's fingers and turned in the breeze to reveal a blue badge with a white logo. It was from a soccer shirt—last seen on Thiago DaSilva.

CHAPTER 48

LET'S SPLIT UP,
AND OTHER DUMB IDEAS

We did exactly what we shouldn't have done: we split up to search for Thiago.

I even heard myself saying, "Good idea, that way we can cover more ground." Hadn't I learned *anything* from watching scary movies?

But I didn't really want to be around both Ellie and Denny right now. Ellie sure, but Denny? Nah.

We agreed to meet back at camp in an hour, hopefully with Thiago in tow. If we hadn't found him by then, the plan was to get everyone else involved. If that failed, we'd have to talk to Brushes and our teachers. There was no other option.

The area I was searching took me in the

direction of the secret ravine. As I got closer I heard something that sounded a lot like it could be Thiago. I kept my head down and crawled to the edge of the rise and looked down at the ravine.

I risked a peek. The sound I'd heard wasn't Thiago. It was someone else.

A lot of someones.

There were six MegaGlobal trucks along with a whole bunch of men in suits, looking at a map spread out across the hood of one of the trucks.

I wished I had a pair of binoculars to get a closer look at that map.

I inched forward. As I did, a large stone came loose and bounced slowly down the hill, getting faster and faster as it got closer to the trucks.

The stone bounced hard on the flat part of the ravine, took a wicked swerve left, and clanged loudly against the fender of a truck.

Everyone in the ravine stopped talking. Then they all looked at the truck and then back up the rise toward me.

I ducked and rolled backward down the hill, my feet scrabbling for balance. I didn't *think* they saw me. Without looking back, I raced back to Camp Culture. Behind me, I heard a truck engine start.

They were after me!

As I ran, I thought about Thiago's shredded soccer shirt, about the croc Brushes McGarrity kept in a cage behind the trailer, about the astonishing amount of money the Brilliant Bluebird might be worth, and about what bad people like MegaGlobal would do to nosy kids who poked around in things that were none of their business.

I ran faster.

CHAPTER 49

URGENT BUTT ISSUE

If you've ever wondered what it would be like to be able to sprint faster than an Olympic gold medalist, I can totally recommend being chased by a giant crocodile and a pack of MegaGlobal henchmen as a surefire way to find out.

Traveling at roughly the speed of light, I covered the distance from the ravine back to Camp Culture in about six seconds flat. With a last glance over my shoulder to check that I'd given them the slip—and unless they'd been strapped to the back of a heat-seeking missile, I was pretty sure I *had*—I hurtled into camp so fast that when I put on the brakes I dug a trench nine feet long.

Okay, maybe I'm exaggerating a little…but I *was* moving pretty fast. I waited a few seconds for my lungs to stop burning and then casually walked into camp.

I was not prepared to see what I saw.

Barry the rock monster was there along with two tough-looking police officers and a couple of regular guys talking to Vern. Yrsa was back from torturing her violin, Vloot was working on his sculpture, and Linda was still quietly folding paper.

And there, sitting to one side of this group at the table and wolfing down a plate of eggs, was Thiago.

I blinked.

Don't get me wrong—I was real glad to see Thiago...I just hadn't *expected* to *ever* see him again.

Ellie and Denny were here, too, I noticed. Somehow they'd gotten back before me.

"What happened?" I asked them.

"Thiago got lost," Denny said. "Had a UBI."

"A UBI?"

"Urgent Butt Issue." Denny pointed at the desert. "When you gotta go, you gotta go. Y'know?"

"Oh," I said. "Uh, yeah."

"Never mind all *that*," Ellie said. "The big news is, Barry called the police and they're going to go out to Crocodile Rocks!"

Denny nodded and smiled. "Barry's buddy on the council pulled a few strings. The MegaGlobal people aren't happy but the police are going anyway."

"What about Brushes?" I asked.

Denny shrugged.

I tried to ignore the weird feeling that came back when I thought about how Ellie and Denny both knew the police had been called, but they'd had to tell me.

I'd had all these chances with Ellie only to blow

them, then Denny came along and now the two of them were keeping things from me? It shouldn't have mattered—what mattered was that the police had been called—but I felt left out.

"This will be epic," Ellie said. "I'm going to film the whole thing."

I nodded, watching her take out her camera. We did it! We'd run around all over the desert, fought crocs, discovered crooks, and all this exciting stuff...

So why did I feel like I had an Urgent Butt Issue of my own?

CHAPTER 50

I HAVE A BAD FEELING ABOUT THIS

When we reached the entrance of Crocodile Rocks the place was deserted. No trucks. No Suits. No henchmen. Nothing.

"I have a bad feeling about this," I said to Ellie, but she wasn't listening. Which was maybe for the best. I wasn't sure if she'd think I was a nerd for accidentally quoting *Star Wars*.

Ellie had her camera out and was circling the scene, trying to get a good angle. If we were right about Crocodile Rocks, this story was going to be *huge*.

Barry, the council members, and the police walked over to the cave entrance. All the Camp

Culture kids gathered round, along with our teachers. For most of them, it was their first sight of Crocodile Rocks. Personally, it was fine by me if I never set foot inside a cave again.

"No sign of activity," one of the cops said, looking at the red dirt. He glanced at Barry. "You say you saw trucks here?"

The rock monster nodded. "Plenty."

"Let's get on with it, Barry," said one of the councilors. "It's a long way back tonight."

"The paintings are about three hundred feet in," Barry said, "as far as I can tell from the photos."

"Get the big flashlight out of the truck, Rollo," one of the cops called. "It's black as coal in here."

As Rollo headed to the truck, everyone else entered the cave. I took a deep breath, then followed them inside.

By the time Rollo got back, we'd all wandered about ten paces inside the cave entrance.

Although you couldn't see far, I got the sense that this cave was much, much bigger than the one near our camp. A truck would have no problem getting inside.

"C'mon," Barry said. "Let's get some light."

Rollo switched on the flashlight and pointed the beam up at the cave walls...

CHAPTER 51

THAT'S IT?

This was what was on the walls:

A big, fat nothing. *Zero, zilch, zip.*

No antelope, no hunters, no crocodiles.
Just a sheer wall of smooth, curved sandstone
disappearing into deep shadow near the cave roof.

"They must be farther back." Barry picked up
the flashlight and ran down the tunnel, the light
dancing as he moved to show blank rock, blank
rock, and same as before, blank rock. "They've
got to be here!" Barry's voice got more and more
puzzled the farther inside the cave he went. He
said some words I can't repeat here.

We followed him another eighty paces or so
down the tunnel until it was obvious that the
whole place was completely, absolutely, 100 percent
empty of anything resembling a cave painting.

"I don't get it," Denny whispered.

Ellie looked like someone had handed her a
really difficult math problem.

I saw the two cops exchange glances. The council members did the same. Linda tapped me on the shoulder and raised her eyebrows questioningly.

Barry came back into view, his expression grim. "They've cleaned it all!" he said. He kicked a stone and said more of those words I can't repeat.

"Overnight?" Rollo said doubtfully.

"This is a big company we're talking about!" Barry retorted. "They could get something like that done easy! MegaGlobal is—"

"We need to be careful, Barry," one of the councilor women said. "MegaGlobal is very powerful. You can't just go flinging around stories without proof."

Barry's head exploded.

Okay, it didn't, but for a second or two, it was a close one.

Barry handed the flashlight back to Rollo.

"That's it?" Denny said. "Just like that?"

I glared at him because he was standing with Ellie.

"That's it," Barry replied, and headed toward the light.

I'd like to be able to tell you that we discovered some other clue out there at Crocodile Rocks and the police dug a little deeper and found out that everything we'd told them was true and they threw us a big party with fireworks.

But, hey! Guess what? That didn't happen.

Vern took us back to the camp, his face as blank as the walls of Crocodile Rocks.

Barry got into a car with the council members and headed back to Bigbottom Creek. Denny stalked off toward the campfire and lay down. From the look on his face, I knew he didn't want company, so even Ellie left him alone.

"What now?" she said to me.

I shook my head. "I guess we do what we came here to do."

CHAPTER 52

FUN. REMEMBER FUN?

Chiaroscuro.

That's what I was painting and drawing. It means working with a lot of very dark areas on the canvas or page. I was mostly creating night scenes of Crocodile Rocks silhouetted by the crisscrossing headlights from the (nonexistent) trucks.

Since it looked like all our amateur detective stuff was leading nowhere, I figured I might as well get something down on paper.

I was pretty excited by the drawings, too. They made me feel as if I was getting somewhere, but I didn't know that what I was doing even *had* a name until Denny told me.

Denny had stayed quiet the day we'd been out to Crocodile Rocks but by the following morning he was back to doing his thing, making a video mash-up about the camp from Ellie's footage and Yrsa's music. Denny got Ellie to film me painting and then put graphics over parts of the project, which was when I learned I was making *chiaroscuro* art.

It looked amazing.

And I guess it was nice of him to include me in his project, even if he and Ellie were working together also. I really wanted to do something about all this, but I didn't know *what*. I felt kind of crummy, though that wasn't Denny's fault. It also wasn't Ellie's fault. But I didn't think it was *mine,* either. It was just how I felt, and I couldn't change it.

All the Camp Culture kids did their own cool stuff that week, getting ready for the exhibit at the end of our trip. Some of them, like Ellie and Denny, worked in teams—of course. Others, like Eric, Monique, and I did our own thing. Vloot kept working on his sculpture of Brushes.

As the days passed, full of art and friends and camping—poop shovels and all—the whole episode of being chased by crocodiles and suspecting that Brushes had faked the paintings in the McGarrity Caves, MegaGlobal, and Barry the rock monster all seemed to fade until there were times I wasn't sure *any* of it had happened.

I mean, I knew the croc was real but I had no actual proof that Brushes had anything to do with that. There was the cage and the stuff Denny had found online, but it didn't add up to real proof.

Those trucks could have been doing something completely innocent. Those paint cans could have been for anything, and we didn't know for sure that Brushes *had* painted the "fake" McGarrity Cave Paintings.

We didn't know any of those things. We just thought we did and I was learning that there's a big difference between the two.

As much as I hate to admit it, maybe there were some things that adults could do better than kids.

CHAPTER 53

A FACE LIKE A SLAPPED TROUT

After ten days in the desert, the Bigbottom Creek Hotel looked like the Monte Carlo Ritz-Carlton.

Running water! Drinks with ice! Showers! BEDS! Plus, we didn't have to poop out in the wilderness!

"I'm so happy my heart might explode!" Linda squeaked, looking around excitedly.

This place was a totally, yes-indeedy, uh-huh-oh-yeah-that's-what-I'm-talking-about, complete six-star *luxury* compared to Camp Culture. In the first few hours after we got back, I had three showers, six naps, and almost overdosed on icy-cold cans of soda.

We were all due to fly out the next day
but before then there was a celebration at the
McGarrity Ranch. Brushes came around in the
afternoon and gave us all presents to remember
Camp Culture by, which made me feel bad about
spying on him.

My present was a pot of paint made from
the red California sand. It was a nice idea but I
had already mixed up a few pots of my own, so
I swapped the paint for Vloot's present—a cool
geode that you could break open to reveal all
these crystals inside. I didn't want to break it yet,
though. I'd save that for later. So right now, it just

looked like an ugly, baseball-shaped rock.

"Nice rock," Ellie said. She'd been given a little framed drawing Brushes had done of an odd-looking rock formation. It was pretty good.

I nodded but didn't say much.

The fact was, Ellie and I were in a weird place. Since we'd got back to the hotel, I kept thinking about it, and I kind of wanted to tell her how I felt. But that didn't seem like the best idea, so I didn't. I gave her the silent treatment instead.

Not my finest idea, but I wasn't exactly known for my smooth way with girls.

Brushes' place was huge. A bit run-down here and there, maybe, but *big*. Along the back of the main house was his art gallery. All the stuff we'd done out at Camp Culture was arranged on the walls and on pedestals along with a whole bunch of stuff by Brushes (which, I had to admit, wasn't bad).

Ellie and Denny's movie was being projected onto a wall in one corner. Yrsa's soundtrack played over the speakers. It still sounded like two cats fighting in a washing machine but somehow it was exactly right for the movie. Pretty much everyone who lived in Bigbottom Creek was there, including the two cops who'd been out to the caves, Barry the rock monster, the entire Bigbottom Creek Council, the Suits, and Brushes. The only face I couldn't see was Vern's.

I watched Ellie talking and laughing with people who weren't me and felt a hot flush of anger. Even though some of the people she was talking to were our teachers, like Mrs. Donatello.

Ellie glanced over in my direction. What I *should* have done was walk over and join in the conversation, make up with Ellie, and enjoy my last evening in California.

What I *did* was turn right around and go out the back door, slamming it behind me as hard as I could.

CHAPTER 54

ROTTEN LUCK WITH GIRLS

Hey, guys, here's a solid bit of Rafe Khatchadorian advice: when making a dramatic exit, there's one Very Important Point to remember—you have to have somewhere to stomp off dramatically *to*.

I had forgotten this Very Important Point, so once I'd left the house I found myself standing in Brushes' backyard in the dark alone and with exactly zero idea about where I was going to go or what I was going to do when I got there.

Being in a bad mood *sucked* and being annoyed at Ellie on the last night at camp *double*-sucked.

But I still didn't want to talk to her, so when she came out after me, I *really* regretted having nowhere to storm off to.

"Hey," she said.

I decided to play it cool.

So I didn't respond.

In retrospect, that was probably pretty rude, but I never claimed I make the best decisions. In fact, my reputation kind of says otherwise.

"What's up with you?" Ellie asked. "You've been really weird."

I shrugged. "Nothing."

Let me tell you something, girls ALWAYS know when you're lying.

"Liar," Ellie said.

See???

But I didn't want to lie to Ellie. I didn't want to argue with her, either. But I couldn't pretend everything was okay because it wasn't.

I was jealous of Denny.

Ellie had been hanging out with him so much recently, and he was a good guy and all, but...it meant she was hanging out less with *me*.

"Come on," Ellie said, punching me in the shoulder. "What's your problem?"

"Noth—"

I stopped. Time to fess up.

Instead, I admitted, "I like you, Ellie. Like, *like you* like you."

Wow, could I say "like" any more? Way to look like an idiot in front of the girl I liked!

There—I did it again. Yeesh!

Love makes you kinda dumb, huh?

"You...what?" Ellie stared at me like I'd said I ate tree bark for breakfast.

"Like you."

Aaaaand again. What's that, six?

"Um..."

Uh-oh. "Um" is never a good sign in these kinds of situations.

"Rafe, I..."

Crud, here it comes. "You know what," I said, "never mind. It's stupid. Forget it. I didn't mean it."

"It's not stupid," she said. "It's just...I think of you as a friend."

"Yeah, I get it," is what I said. But what I was thinking was, *Friend-zoned TWICE*. First Jeanne, then Ellie. I really had rotten luck with girls.

I, Rafe Khatchadorian, am officially never going to like another girl again!

CHAPTER 55

THE DOG THAT WASN'T A DOG

I'm sorry," Ellie said.

"It's fine." I shrugged.

She looked like she might say something else, so I added, "You should go back inside. I'll be there in a minute."

"Oh, okay…"

I thought maybe she'd refuse. And maybe—just maybe!—she'd even tell me she'd been kidding and she *like* liked me, too! Then we could laugh about how silly we'd both been this whole time being afraid to tell each other how we felt.

...and they all lived happily ever after!

But I'm sure you know that's not what happened.

Instead, Ellie turned around and went back inside. She didn't even make sure I was really coming in, too.

She just left.

As I stood there wondering what to do, I heard a whistle followed by a series of muffled *thuds*.

There was something off about those thuds. I'd heard them before but I couldn't remember exactly where. The sounds were coming from a big shed near the main house.

Curious, I moved closer. Vern was standing outside it, holding a stick. As I watched, he threw the stick and a dog bounced out of the shed, its tail wagging in excitement.

I stopped dead. I'd found out what was making those weirdly familiar thudding noises.

But that dog was no dog.

It was a crocodile.

The same crocodile I'd stood on in the desert!

A lot of things went through my mind at the same time. Here they are, in no particular order:

1. We were *right* about Brushes all along! He was in this—whatever "this" was—up to his bristly neck.
2. That croc was *way* bigger than I remember.
3. Crocs like playing fetch—who knew?
4. Brushes had been using the pet croc to keep people from snooping at Crocodile Rocks.
5. If Brushes was crooked, why was he running a kids' art camp?

The answer to the last one of those questions came to me first. Brushes was using us as cover. He was here for some other reason but wanted to keep it a secret. The question was, what?

I tried to concentrate. If…

Uh-oh.

The croc had stopped playing with Vern. Both of them were looking right at me.

It was a bad moment.

CHAPTER 56

FETCH

My eyes met the eyes of the croc. Time stood still.

For a long moment we just looked at each other. I didn't have the slightest doubt that the croc recognized me as the kid who'd used him as a living pedestal.

Then I heard Vern say something. It was the first complete word I'd ever heard him say and it gave me an electric jolt that started in my brain and shot down the length of my body. It was the scariest word I had ever heard.

Fetch.

Being a toy for a monster crocodile is not something I wanted to try. But I did have two things on my side:

1. I had a fifty-foot head start.
2. I had been in this situation before.

Spinning into a one-eighty, I sprinted across the yard and hightailed it straight for the house. If you've ever been in some sort of accident, you'll know that being in great danger does something different to time. Everything gets real *slooooow*. Every detail becomes Ultra-HD sharp. And your brain starts doing strange things.

Example: instead of thinking *only* about escaping from a monster crocodile, my brain was figuring out the last few details of Brushes' plan.

The reason Brushes was running this art camp was because he needed a reason to hang around the caves all the time while he looked for the

Brilliant Bluebird Diamond. He'd drawn those fake cave paintings to keep MegaGlobal away. The caves would be protected thanks to the "Native American artwork," and MegaGlobal's search for the diamond would stop. With the paintings, this place would be off-limits to their mining. He must've known where the diamond was—or been pretty sure about it. Maybe he'd been involved in the heist, or he was working for someone who had been. Which meant the diamond was nearby.

Maybe nearer than any of us suspected.

After all, the cave paintings were gone now. That meant Brushes was done looking. And that might also mean...

He found the diamond.

I thought of Vloot's sculpture of McGarrity, which you might think is a weird thing considering what was happening. But it had always seemed majorly strange that Brushes wanted a sculpture of himself. Except now that I knew what was happening...what better way to smuggle the Brilliant Bluebird out of the caves than by stuffing it inside some kid's arts and crafts project? Everyone was looking for it, but no one would be looking for it in a sculpture. It was genius.

I figured all that out in the time it took me to get halfway to the house.

Glancing back, I saw that the croc was gaining.

I put on an extra spurt and reached the door. I heard that familiar *boofboom! boofboom!* getting closer and closer.

Ten feet to go.

Boofboom!

Five.

Boofboom!

Two. I reached for the handle...

Boofboom!

I yanked open the door.

CHAPTER 57

SOMETIMES YOU GOTTA DO WHAT YOU GOTTA DO

CROC!" I yelled as I skidded into the gallery. "CROC! CROC! CROC! CROC! CRRRRRROOOOOOOCC!"

It was safe to say that I had everyone's undivided attention.

I didn't care. All I cared about was getting as far away as possible from the croc. I'd seen the look in that thing's eye. The croc was not going to let me get away twice.

I hurdled the first display table and zigzagged through the crowd. It was only when I was on my second lap of the gallery that I figured something out.

The croc wasn't here.

I jogged to a halt, scanning the gallery in case it was hiding behind a painting.

"Rafe?" Mrs. Donatello asked.

"Are you okay?" Ellie said.

Of everyone in here, they were the only two not laughing, even though I wouldn't have blamed them—especially Ellie after I blurted out that I liked her earlier.

Everyone's got a boiling point and mine had just been reached.

Sometimes a Khatchadorian's gotta do what a Khatchadorian's gotta do. I took a few paces toward the plinth holding the sculpture of Brushes McGarrity.

"Sorry, Vloot," I said, looking at him.

"What for?" Vloot asked.

"For this," I said, and knocked the sculpture of Brushes onto the floor, where it smashed into a thousand pieces.

A gigantic blue diamond skids across the floor of the gallery and comes to rest at the feet of the astonished Bigbottom Creek Police Chief.

Everyone freezes and looks at Brushes McGarrity.

"You darn kids," he snarls. "If you hadn't interfered with our crafty scheme to smuggle the stolen Brilliant Bluebird Diamond out of California, I'd have gotten away!"

Except, this wasn't the movies, so none of that happened.

In fact, McGarrity didn't say anything, mainly because when Vloot's sculpture hit the deck, no hidden diamond came out.

I'd been 100 percent, completely wrong.

Oops.

CHAPTER 58

TIME TO GET OUTTA HERE!

Everyone looked at me. I wanted to come out with some kind of wisecrack but I couldn't think of anything that sounded right.

So I did what anyone would do—I *ran*.

I had no idea what I was going to do once I got outside, but even facing a vengeful crocodile was better than staying in the gallery with everyone laughing at me. I hit the gas and took off like a rocket.

Unfortunately, I'd forgotten that the floor was covered in thousands of bits of Vloot's broken sculpture. My right foot landed on Brushes McGarrity's clay nose and I skidded across the shiny polished floor like a first-time ice-skater whose pants were full of wasps.

"Neeeeeyarrrrrrr!!" I yelled, and slammed
headfirst into Eric's artwork: a big net woven from
bits of wool that was hanging from the ceiling. I
bounced back and crashed awkwardly to the floor.
My souvenir geode also crashed to the floor—I
thought it might break, but it didn't—along with
a bunch of other stuff from Brushes' table. Objects
rained on my head, including some crystals and
something that felt like a boulder. I glared at it and
realized it was another geode.

I snatched mine off the floor, then I got up and
then fell down. Then I did it again.

Ellie screamed and I looked down to see my foot pointing the wrong way.

I blinked. I was used to both my feet pointing the same way—forward.

And then two things hit me at the same time. First, that I had just broken my leg. And second, a tidal wave of pain. I opened my mouth to scream.

Then everything went black.

CHAPTER 59

BROKEN LEGS HURT... AND OTHER REALLY OBVIOUS THINGS

I ended up in the hospital. Which meant everyone at Camp Culture left without me. Which meant I didn't get to say a proper good-bye to Ellie. Which meant the last real conversation we had was me making a fool out of myself telling her that I *like* liked her. Ugh!

I decided I'd text her.

Later.

Once I figured out what to say.

Another layer of experience settled on me like dust. I was building up a pretty thick crust now and it was *painful*.

That's the thing about getting experience—you

have to get cut before it becomes a scar. Experience isn't always fun. Experience can hurt. Endings hurt. Being humiliated at the gallery hurt. Ellie not liking me back *hurt*. And my broken leg *really* hurt.

Not like when it happened—that had been *waaaaay* beyond painful—but now it had settled into a kind of dull ache. And the thing itched like crazy.

But cast or no cast, I'm not sitting in this hospital while Brushes gets away!

I tie the bedsheets into a rope and scale the side of the building in no time at all. It's like I'm a total pro.

In less than ten minutes, I'm out of the hospital—freedom! At last!

Then I head back to the caves and find the Brilliant Bluebird, turn it in to the police, and save the day.

Now THAT'S an ending, huh?

CHAPTER 60

WEAR AND TEAR

What, you actually believed me? You thought THAT was the ending? Are you nuts? No way could I have found the Brilliant Bluebird. And *especially* no way I was scaling down the wall of the hospital with a broken leg and a rope made from bedsheets.

Even if I hadn't been stuck in the hospital, I wouldn't have found the diamond in the caves.

It wasn't there.

Remember at the beginning, when I said someone would break into my bedroom to steal the diamond? Well, we're almost up to that part. Be patient!

A week after I got back home, I was lying on my bed in the middle of the night, looking at the moonlit ceiling, and trying not to think about the itch on my leg that was keeping me awake.

The ceiling seemed smooth at first, but then I started seeing all the little flaws in the paint: a crack here, a scrap of a spider's web there. The longer I looked, the more cracks I saw until it seemed that pretty much most of the bedroom ceiling was about to fall in. But it wasn't—it was still the same old ceiling just with a bit more wear and tear.

Like me.

I was a different Rafe Khatchadorian from the one who'd left Hills Village a few weeks ago. Bigbottom Creek had left its marks.

Some of them—like the broken leg, and the scrapes on my elbows I'd gotten from squeezing into the caves at Crocodile Rocks—were easy to see. The rest weren't visible, but they were still there, all right. Like running into Brushes McGarrity's gallery, yelling "CROCODILE!" at the top of my voice—that was right at the top of my list of embarrassing moments and had left a little scar. Along with telling Ellie I *like* liked her.

That was at the top of the list.

A lot of the other marks you couldn't see were to do with Ellie, too. But some of them were because another Khatchadorian adventure had come to an end.

And one of them was because I was back home.

That felt *wrong*. Me feeling bad about being home, I mean. I felt guilty I wasn't more excited about seeing Mom and Georgia and Grandma Dotty and Junior. Don't get me wrong—it was great seeing them again (especially Junior) and they were making a big fuss about my leg and all... It just wasn't as much fun as the things I'd been doing in California. And we hadn't even visited Hollywood!

There was a noise at my bedroom window. It was a tiny noise. The kind of noise a branch of a tree might make when it brushed the windowsill.

Except we didn't have any trees next to the house.

CHAPTER 61

HiDDEN iN PLAiN SiGHT

I hopped across to the window as best I could, keeping my head down. The noise I'd heard was a ladder being put in place very quietly and very carefully against the side of the house. Through the open window I could hear someone beginning to climb.

Whoever it was moved real slow and quiet.

Burglars!

I was just about to start yelling when I saw something shift out by the edge of our yard. It was a figure dressed all in black, standing in the shadows of the house next door. I couldn't see much but right then the guy turned and caught a patch of light. That was when I saw it—poking out from under the brim of his cap was a bushy beard that, even from this distance, could only belong to one guy.

Brushes McGarrity.

I glanced across to the geode I'd swapped with Vloot and then dropped on the floor. And everything fell into place—all of it, all at once, every last detail.

The Brilliant Bluebird was sitting right there on my bedside.

And Brushes McGarrity was here to get it.

The diamond was never in Vloot's sculpture.

Brushes had found it in the caves all right, but smuggling it away in a piece of art had never been the plan.

Brushes was going to smuggle it inside a geode, until I messed things up by knocking everything off his desk, and accidentally taking the wrong one home with me.

Time stopped.

I had seconds to decide what to do before Vern—who else could it be on the ladder?—reached my room. I thought about Mom and Georgia and Grandma Dotty and how desperate and dangerous McGarrity had to be to come all this way and break into our house. So instead of yelling out, I came up with a plan.

A good one.

Trust me.

HOW TO BREATHE

You never really notice how weird your breathing is until a giant smuggler breaks into your room in the dead of night. I was trying so hard to convince Vern I was fast asleep I started snoring like my life depended on it—which it probably did. I sounded like a dying rhino with asthma, so I toned it way down until I only sounded like a rhino who'd been out jogging. It seemed to do the trick.

I have to admit, Vern made a pretty good burglar. I mean, I don't have that much—or *any*—experience with burglars, but for such a massive guy, he hardly made a sound. Even so, I still knew *exactly* where he was.

It reminded me of this time I was at my desk

in school drawing a picture of Principal Stricker. Somehow, I *knew* she'd materialized somewhere behind me and I turned the page *just* before she could see. A few seconds later and she'd have bitten my head clean off.

That was what it was like now. The exact same spidey sense took over and I could *feel* Vern moving around my room like a great big burglar gorilla.

I risked a peek and, through my one half-open eye, I saw Vern looking right at me.

I swallowed a lump that felt like it was the size of the Brilliant Bluebird Diamond.

Here goes nothing.

I sat up, then pulled one arm out from under my blanks and held up...

Junior's squeaky toy.

Yup, you read that right. I was holding Junior's doggy toy. I squeaked that thing as loud as I could.

Vern stared at me like I had an octopus sitting on my head.

And stared.

And *stared*.

I began to sweat and think maybe I'd made a major Khatchadorian boo-boo by trying to be too clever. Who did I think I was—some kind of criminal mastermind? *Vern could finish me off at any moment.*

That's when my bedroom door finally burst open and Junior raced in.

I squeaked the toy again and Junior ran straight under Vern's legs on the way to get the toy. Vern fell to the floor...hard.

Yes!

But he wasn't down for the count yet.

Junior leaped onto my bed, wanting his toy badly. That's when I pulled out my *other* arm from under the blankets. I held a backpack, and in that backpack was the Brilliant Bluebird Diamond. Junior sniffed it, then went back to jumping at me for his toy.

"Hold *still*," I whispered, struggling to get the backpack on him.

Vern groaned and got to his feet. He glared at me and started for the bed.

Just in time, I finished with the backpack.

Then I hurled Junior's squeaky toy out into the hall.

Junior took off, a blur of fur and backpack zipping out the door. Vern ran after him.

Now I know you're probably thinking that wasn't a smart idea, because now Vern was in our house and he might wake up my mom or grandma or Georgia. But I told you, I had a plan.

And it wasn't over yet.

CHAPTER 63

THE ACTUAL END

So while Vern was chasing Junior around the house, the cops were on their way. They'd just *happened* to get an anonymous tip that the famous, missing Brilliant Bluebird Diamond was nearby.

And that *maybe* they'd find it in our front yard.

And guess what? They did.

I managed to hobble down the stairs and open the front door, then Vern chased Junior right out into the yard—

—and right into the sight of the cops as they pulled their cars into our driveway.

There were lots of sirens and lights, which woke up Mom, Grandma Dotty, and Georgia. The cops arrested Vern and Brushes, who was waiting nearby in a car. They took the Brilliant Bluebird, and it was all amazing, like something out of a movie, only this was *real*.

I texted everyone from Camp Culture about it the next day, including Denny.

What? I wasn't jealous of him anymore.

So then Denny told Barry the rock monster. Barry and some of his activist buddies got a freeze on any more digging activity out at the caves. Because of all the publicity about the Brilliant Bluebird, the caves got pretty famous, and real Native American artwork was discovered, so mining came to a dead halt.

This is the best one: I got invited back to California once my leg's all fixed. Someone wants to give me an award or whatever. I think they want to make me "Lord Khatchadorian" or "Governor Khatchadorian" or something super-cool like that. It'd be great. I'll even get to go to Hollywood this time!

Okay, okay, I'm kidding. There's no huge award

or anything, and I'm not sure when I'll get to visit Hollywood.

But maybe I can convince Mom to plan us a trip. Then I'd be able to see Ellie again.

I texted her about this whole thing, too, and we're cool now. I'm probably still going to make a fool of myself in front of her—and a lot of other people in the future—but that's just how I am. I do stupid things, and I get into trouble.

But hey, sometimes it helps find a missing diamond!

Anyway, my next mission is to convince Mom about that Hollywood thing. Wish me luck!

(And yes, this really is the end now!)

Read the Middle School series

Visit the **Middle School world** on the Penguin website
to find out more! **www.penguin.co.uk**

THE MIDDLE SCHOOL SERIES

THE WORST YEARS OF MY LIFE
(with Chris Tebbetts)

This is the insane story of my first year at middle school, when I, Rafe Khatchadorian, took on a real-life bear (sort of), sold my soul to the school bully, and fell for the most popular girl in school. Come join me, if you dare…

GET ME OUT OF HERE!
(with Chris Tebbetts)

We've moved to the big city, where I'm going to a super-fancy art school. The first project is to create something based on our exciting lives. But my life is TOTALLY BORING. It's time for Operation Get a Life.

MY BROTHER IS A BIG, FAT LIAR
(with Lisa Papademetriou)

So you've heard all about my big brother, Rafe, and now it's time to set the record straight. (Almost) EVERYTHING he says is a Big, Fat Lie. I'm Georgia, and it's time for some payback…Khatchadorian style.

HOW I SURVIVED BULLIES, BROCCOLI, AND SNAKE HILL
(with Chris Tebbetts)

I'm excited for a fun summer at camp—until I find out it's a summer *school* camp. There's no fun and games here, just a whole lotta trouble!

ULTIMATE SHOWDOWN
(with Julia Bergen)

Who would have thought that we—Rafe and Georgia—would ever agree on anything? That's right—we're writing a book together. And the best part? We want you to be part of the fun too!

SAVE RAFE!
(with Chris Tebbetts)

I'm in worse trouble than ever! I need to survive a gut-bustingly impossible outdoor excursion so I can return to school next year. But will I get through in one piece?

JUST MY ROTTEN LUCK
(with Chris Tebbetts)

I'm heading back to Hills Village Middle School, but only if I take "special" classes... If that wasn't bad enough, when I somehow land a place on the school football team, I find myself playing alongside the biggest bully in school, Miller the Killer!

DOG'S BEST FRIEND
(with Chris Tebbetts)

It's a dog-eat-dog world. When I started my own dog-walking empire, I didn't think it could go so horribly wrong! Somehow, I always seem to end up in deep doo-doo...

ESCAPE TO AUSTRALIA
(with Martin Chatterton)
I just won an all-expenses paid trip of a lifetime to Australia. But here's the bad news: I MIGHT NOT MAKE IT OUT ALIVE!

FROM HERO TO ZERO
(with Chris Tebbetts)
I'm going on the class trip of a lifetime! What could possibly go wrong? I've spent all of middle school being chased by Miller the Killer, but on this trip, there's NOWHERE TO RUN!

BORN TO ROCK
(with Chris Tebbetts)
My brother, Rafe Khatchadorian, has been public enemy #1 my whole life. But if I want to win the Battle of the Bands, I'm going to have to recruit the most devious person I know...

MASTER OF DISASTER
(with Chris Tebbetts)
My buddy Jimmy and I are throwing a huge festival dedicated to BOOKS! But when one tiiiiiny problem snowballs into a BIG one, everyone's gotta work together so the party doesn't get shut down—PERMANENTLY!

ALSO BY JAMES PATTERSON

DOG DIARIES SERIES
Dog Diaries (*with Steven Butler*)
Happy Howlidays! (*with Steven Butler*)
Mission Impawsible (*with Steven Butler*)
Curse of the Mystery Mutt (*with Steven Butler*)
Camping Chaos! (*with Steven Butler*)

THE I FUNNY SERIES
I Funny (*with Chris Grabenstein*)
I Even Funnier (*with Chris Grabenstein*)
I Totally Funniest (*with Chris Grabenstein*)
I Funny TV (*with Chris Grabenstein*)
School of Laughs (*with Chris Grabenstein*)
The Nerdiest, Wimpiest, Dorkiest I Funny Ever
(*with Chris Grabenstein*)

MAX EINSTEIN SERIES
The Genius Experiment (*with Chris Grabenstein*)
Rebels with a Cause (*with Chris Grabenstein*)
Saves the Future (*with Chris Grabenstein*)

TREASURE HUNTERS SERIES
Treasure Hunters (*with Chris Grabenstein*)
Danger Down the Nile (*with Chris Grabenstein*)
Secret of the Forbidden City (*with Chris Grabenstein*)
Peril at the Top of the World (*with Chris Grabenstein*)
Quest for the City of Gold (*with Chris Grabenstein*)
All-American Adventure (*with Chris Grabenstein*)
The Plunder Down Under (*with Chris Grabenstein*)

HOUSE OF ROBOTS SERIES
House of Robots (*with Chris Grabenstein*)
Robots Go Wild! (*with Chris Grabenstein*)
Robot Revolution (*with Chris Grabenstein*)

JACKY HA-HA SERIES
Jacky Ha-Ha (*with Chris Grabenstein*)
My Life is a Joke (*with Chris Grabenstein*)

OTHER ILLUSTRATED NOVELS
Kenny Wright: Superhero (*with Chris Tebbetts*)
Homeroom Diaries (*with Lisa Papademetriou*)
Word of Mouse (*with Chris Grabenstein*)
Pottymouth and Stoopid (*with Chris Grabenstein*)
Laugh Out Loud (*with Chris Grabenstein*)
Not So Normal Norbert (*with Joey Green*)
Unbelievably Boring Bart (*with Duane Swierczynski*)
Katt vs. Dogg (*with Chris Grabenstein*)

For more information about James Patterson's novels,
visit www.penguin.co.uk